Other Books by John Becker

THE NEGRO IN AMERICAN LIFE

For Children

MELINDY'S MEDAL, with Georgene Faulkner

NEW FEATHERS FOR THE OLD GOOSE

NEW TRAGEDY AT THE WATERFALL

JAIMIE

JAIMIE

An Autobiographical Novel
in Short Stories

by John Becker

David R. Godine · Publisher · Boston

First U.S. edition published in 1981 by
David R. Godine, Publisher, Inc.
306 Dartmouth Street
Boston, Massachusetts 02116

Previously published as *After Geneva* in a somewhat different form in 1975
by London Magazine Editions Ltd.

Library of Congress Cataloging in Publication Data
Becker, John Leonard, 1901–
  Jaimie.
  Edition of 1975 published under title : After Geneva.
  CONTENTS : Three sisters and a horse.—Jaimie.—Poor
Hubert.—[etc.]
  I. Title.
PZ4.B39515Jai   1981   [PS3552.E256]   813¹.54   80–65424
ISBN 0–87923–340–0

Manufactured in the United States of America

Contents

Three Sisters and a Horse

Gladys was the oldest one and there was always something sweet about her besides the scent of lingerie. She was my favorite one and the most important one too because it was she who made up the game.

Flo was the second one, the very dark one, and she and Jessie, the youngest one, had the bodies of dancers and there was always an excitement about them too and at the Charity Reviews they were the best things in them and could have gone on the stage. I knew, not so much from what I saw, but from what they told me. I thought Gladys was the most beautiful one but then, as I was only five, I thought they were all beautiful.

I went every Thursday on my nurse's day off. The good time began at the start. Whoever opened the door would call, "Jaimie's here" and the others would come running, all of them with the sweet smell of lingerie. Flo, the dark one, would unbutton my coat and Jessie, the littlest one, the thin one, would bounce me in the air and they'd fuss over me and kiss me and say, "Jaimie, where'd you get those pretty blue eyes?" and "Where'd you get your curly hair?" and Gladys, the oldest one, my favorite one, who smelt the sweetest of all, would put her head down on my stomach so gently as if she was afraid something would break and say, "Sssh, everybody. Yes, it's talking, it wants its lunch."

Because I liked it lunch was always the same: noodles, chicken salad with surprises like grapes and pineapple in it, and ice cream, only the ice cream was different. The joke was always the same, though, "Sorry, Jaimie, no ice cream today" and then it would come in – an ice cream chicken with different colored ice cream eggs or a butterfly and once there was a melon, green on the outside, vanilla for the white, strawberry for the red, and the seeds were chocolate.

Sometimes Cousin Milton, the sisters' father, came home for lunch and afterwards he would take me aside to whisper embarrassing questions like "Are you married? How many children have you now? And how do you support them?" and the sisters would laugh but I always wondered why such nice girls had such a foolish father. Once he got mad at Gladys and started yelling at her about lingerie. He said, "It's no place for a little boy anyway. Take him out to the park."

Because what the sisters really liked was the fitting-changing-trying-on of lingerie. Everything was very fine and sheer and silky and see-through and scented with rosebuds in sweet colors. Gladys wore pink, her soft flesh through chiffon, Flo black with purple and Jessie blue. What is your favorite color, Jaimie? There were laces and silks and ribbbons and pin-cushions with covered buttons, all smelling of perfume, not just Gladys' but everybody's. Everything came from Cousin Milton's store. There was a big mirror and another mirror over the dressing table. They were always changing, naked for a minute, then changing again, looking at each other in the mirrors but each one liked looking at herself best. They would ask me how I liked this or that and what should go where and then they'd laugh and I'd laugh too. They were always kissing each other and kissing me and I'd kiss them back. Rosebuds and breasts and sweet kisses, like ice cream, vanilla and strawberry. Which one do you like best, Jaimie? Gladys. How old was she then? Fifteen . . . sweet fifteen. Once there was some joke when I got under the double chiffon of her nightgown and so much laughter that I was carried away with clowning and took other night-gowns and stuffs and buried myself in them. Then suddenly I was over-come by the excitement or the body scent or the perfume or the heat or perhaps too there was a stoppage of air. I came to with the sisters around me and Jessie had a cold cloth on my head. That was the end of the fun in the lingerie room.

It was after that that Gladys made up the game. She and Flo took Jessie's and my clothes off and our shoes too. They put an old dress on Jessie and tore it up. Then Flo made me pants with a patch; instead of my belt there was a string. Jessie danced and cried because she was so thin. I wanted to dance too but Gladys said no, I could sing. She had the record *Parlez-moi d'Amour*; it was her favorite and we played it all the time and she taught me to sing it just like the Frenchman through my nose. Gladys and Flo put on their hats and walked around the parlour, talking to each other and pretending they were outside.

2

When they came to me they'd stop and put money in the cup and say, "Oh, what a darling little boy" and everytime I'd say, "Merci, bless you" and they'd laugh and I'd laugh too. What was funny was that I said, "Merci, bless you" just like another Frenchman on another record who couldn't speak English right. Gladys said that after we got outside and if people asked if I was French, I wasn't allowed to say anything but "Oui" and Jessie wasn't allowed to say anything at all and if people talked to Jessie I was to put my finger on my forehead and shake my head. This meant Jessie was crazy. I could smile but I could not laugh, after we got outside, she meant; we laughed all the time in the parlour. Before we went Gladys showed me, at the end of the song, how to put my hand over my heart.

We sneaked down the backstairs, but in the vestibule, before going out, we promised on our honor and shook hands on it, the way Gladys told us to, that we wouldn't ever tell anyone about the begging game because it was a secret. Then we sneaked down the alley into the park where Flo put dirt on our faces and hands and on our feet too. I was so happy without my shoes and with the patch and because it was so exciting and a secret. When we came to where the stores were Gladys and Flo left us and Jessie began to dance. She never stopped; she danced something called the time step and she could dance and cry at the same time and when the tears ran down they smeared the dirt. I held out the cup and sang *Parlez-moi* with my hand over my heart the way Gladys showed me. People put money in the cup whether I sang or not but more when I sang and they'd pat me and when they asked if I was French I'd say, "Oui, merci, bless you". If they asked where I lived I'd point to the park. We always made a lot of money but more outside the toyshop until the man came out and gave us money to go away. But we went back again anyway because children on their way in the shop liked to put money in the cup and they'd ask their mothers to put it in coming out too. Sometimes Jessie would dance over to see what was in the cup but I didn't like that. I'd say, "Go away, crazy" but if she said, "Let me see" I'd have to because she wasn't allowed to talk. When it was cold I had an old scarf and a torn sweater and torn shoes and Jessie had shoes too. She didn't need a sweater; it kept her warm dancing all the time. Sometimes Gladys watched us from the corner and when it got late she was always waiting in the park with our coats and then we'd sneak back to the house where Flo would have my bath ready. I never liked my bath at home but Flo's was lovely smelling like pine trees. And afterwards we had the party because we always had a party after the game. We saved the ice cream for it and there was more chicken salad and cake too and hot chocolate and other things and Gladys put the money in the middle of the table and everybody kissed everybody and after we were filled up we'd count it and everybody was so excited that everybody kissed everybody again and Flo wrote down in a book all the pennies and nickels and dimes and quarters and sometimes there were dollar bills and once somebody gave us more! Gladys called me, "Jaimie, the little king of the beggars". I never wanted to go home. I was so happy with them I wanted to live there.

The begging game ended when we were arrested. A policeman followed us to the park where we were caught in the act: Gladys was buttoning on my coat. She was probably frightened and didn't want me to be, for she kept on kissing me and saying, "Everything'll be all right, Jaimie; it's just for fun". Everything wasn't all right later, but she kept her promise about the fun.

It seems that we had been denounced by the toyshop owner and that the police had arrested us without enthusiasm, for those were the gangster days in Chicago and they had other things to do. Nor did they know what to do with us at the station, because, as we were minors, they couldn't release us until we were identified and for this purpose my father was called from his office down-town. None of this was of much interest to Jessie and me; what concerned us was the time he took in coming, for we were starving, naturally enough after performing and with the party in mind. The captain made us tea but it was as nothing, and so Gladys telephoned Flo, who in due course arrived with a hamper. In it, I like to think, was another ice cream chicken with colored eggs. In any case there was enough to invite the captain to join us and he lent me his gun, and then, by way of returning the courtesy, Gladys suggested that Jessie and I perform. We were happy to oblige; we had eaten, I had the gun, we knew we were good. The captain thought so too; in fact he was so carried away that he invited in the entire force for a repeat performance. It was at this point, while Jessie was crying her crocodile tears and I singing my love song, one hand with the gun and the other over my heart, that my father arrived. During the applause I remember my surprise when he picked me up, not at his being there, but at his show of affection, for he was

4

not a man who often showed his feelings, not with me at any rate. Doubtless he was more surprised than I, for he was amazed by my singing, in French too, as he couldn't imagine where I'd learned it, and by my nonchalance, for he had no way of knowing that I'd been performing to a responsive public for months, but most of all he was impressed when the captain told him that, as we had been watched for some time, it was his opinion that our take was enormous. As an able lawyer, my father would have dismissed this as hearsay, but the evidence was there, in Gladys' drawer, as she informed him when we left the station and she informed him too that it was due to my gift at begging. It may be that my father mistook this for the promise of a gift of money; in any event, together with my performance at the police station, it so delighted him that he talked about it at home and everywhere.

It was his talk at home that undid me. For my mother took a quite different point of view. I didn't know why until after the punishment. I knew I had done nothing to deserve it, for otherwise she would have said that I had. On my nurse's day off I wasn't allowed to go to the sisters.

"Why?"

"Well, they're away."

"Where'd they go?"

"I don't know."

And again on the following Thursday. It didn't ring true.

Miss Holt came on Thursdays but I wasn't allowed to bother her because she had so much to do. While she was fitting sometimes I played on the floor but mother was interested in her neckline. Like the sisters, only not like the sisters at all. They liked to know what I liked. Miss Holt kept the pins in her mouth and if mother asked her something all she could say was, "Mm–, mm–." Once she had to take them out, though. That was when she was changing mother's dress and I said, "I don't like your lingerie." They both laughed and laughed until mother said, "What do you know about lingerie?" but I didn't answer. After a while they didn't know if I was there or not.

I'm sure I didn't think it out. I just went. I knew the way, down Woodlawn to 51st.

There was no one home. I sat there crying – I don't know for how long – until Cousin Milton found me. Later he told my father that I was inconsolable, for he tried to bribe me with ice cream and the merry-go-round at Sans Souci, but all I did was shake my head. Finally he must have taken my sorrow seriously, because when he sat down with me he didn't ask if I was married or how many children I had but he talked to me and I listened, for no one had ever talked to me that way before. He said he understood my loving the sisters, he loved them too, they were lovely girls, but that some day he wouldn't see them either, they'd get married and go away. He said these things happen. He said they hadn't gone away yet, though, it wasn't true, that my mother didn't love the girls the way he and I did and that she had been angry about the begging game and that was why I couldn't come any more. For a while anyway. But he would speak with my father and perhaps she would change her mind. When he stopped talking I thought he wasn't such a foolish man after all.

On my way home he took me to the toyshop and said I could choose anything I wanted. I went over and patted a big black horse with real horse-hair for mane and tail. He was so beautiful I didn't really believe Cousin Milton meant that I could have him until he paid the man and asked, "What are you going to call him?". When I said "Gladys" Cousin Milton said that I'd called him by the right name and another thing, I could always be with this Gladys. He was a pure black horse and so big that when we got home Cousin Milton had to help me carry him up the steps. When our cook opened the door she was surprised about everything – to see Gladys, and to see Cousin Milton, and that I'd been away.

My mother said Gladys was no name for a horse, she said it was an awful name but I called him Gladys anyway.

I lugged him everywhere. That was how my father and mother found out I was listening. They were in the den talking so loud that I woke up. I took Gladys and went down outside the door to listen. The door wasn't closed right; we could see the light coming through.

My father and mother were angry. They were talking about Gladys, both Gladyses, first one and then the other. My mother said that he was taking Gladys', the real Gladys' side because she was a relative.

"Not at all," my father said. "I'm taking Jaimie's side. I'm telling you what Milton told me."

"Did he tell you she was trying to ruin his health as well as his morals? Barefooted in the streets . . ."

6

"There's nothing the matter with his health. It was his affection for the girls that Milton was talking about. And theirs for him. I saw it myself at the police station. You should have seen how sweet Gladys was with him."

"Do you mean I'm not!?"

"I mean they make him feel they want his company. You obviously don't. At least Gladys isn't so busy with her dressmaker that she doesn't know where he is. You didn't even know he'd gone away. Why do you have your dressmaker on the nurse's day out anyway?"

My mother began to cry.

"The trouble with you is that you're jealous of her."

This made my mother stop crying. "Of her!" She was furious.

"Why do you think you get so upset when he calls his horse after her? Milton told me that . . ."

"Oh, Milton, Milton, Milton," my mother said and that was all I heard because I fell asleep on Gladys and he fell in the door and I fell in after him.

Jaimie

Jaimie liked to sit next to Schultz better than anything; of course better than being with Bessie because, well, he was too old for Bessie now; better than with Phelps and the other boys although he liked them too but they didn't know and Schultz did; better than with his father although his father was such a fine lawyer that he was elected to the board of the National Bank of the Republic and a good golfer and popular both with men and women; and better than with his mother, who was lovely and so refined that she knew not only about gardens but had studied Chinese art a little too and was on civic committees like garbage disposal and was charming and a best bridge player and dressed beautifully always. Because of all these things Jaimie couldn't at first understand why he wanted to be with Schultz so much. He knew it was wrong because his mother and father didn't like it and he felt bad about it but he just couldn't help it.

Schultz told Jaimie that he shouldn't be telling him these things, that Jaimie's father should and that if he had a boy like Jaimie he'd want to talk to him.

Jaimie said he guessed his father didn't have the time with the office and board meetings and things like that.

Schultz said his brother ran two barber shops and sometimes wasn't home until midnight and still had time to talk to Schultz's nephew – and he didn't have a wonderful chauffeur to drive him around either. Jaimie laughed. Schultz said his brother had told his nephew everything.

"Everything! ?"

"Yes, everything." Schultz's nephew was thirteen and knew everything.

Ha, ha. Jaimie was only twelve and knew almost everything.

Schultz was twenty-eight, hairy, dark, stocky with full lips. Had he been a boxer his nose would have been punched in.

Before he became a chauffeur, he had been a taxi driver. Chicago was wide open in those days, the red light district with houses along South State. Some of them gave free shows downstairs, not just strip-teases always either like now.

"Whatdyamean?"

Well, Schultz had seen a girl once, after she'd stripped, say, "Who wants me? If you're a man, come up and take me. It's for free."

"Did anyone go?"

"Sure."

"Who?"

"Oh, a big bozo . . . like a yokel or a miner."

"Why did she do it?"

"To get business. It excited the men and then afterwards they'd go upstairs."

"Did you go?"

"No, I didn't have to get mine that way."

When Schultz was twenty-one he drove his cab nights. He used to call for a woman at one of the houses. She was a madame. She lived in the old Dakota Hotel.

She always tipped him nice. Then once, after she'd paid him, she said, "You're a good-looking boy. Why don't you come up and see me?"

So he parked his cab and went up. She told him, "If you want to be good, you've got to know how." She knew too. He used to go and see her regular after that. She was very clean. She taught him everything.

"What?"

"Oh," Schultz laughed, "that would be telling."

Schultz said he could control every muscle he had. He said that he'd worked out in a gym, that it took a long time but he could control every muscle in his body.

"*Every* muscle?"

"Yes, *every* muscle."

Jaimie sat with Schultz all the time, outside the house, while his mother was shopping, waiting at his father's office, riding downtown and back or to the club in the country.

His father said that he was with Schultz too much. He asked what they talked about.

"Oh, I don't know."

"Well, what?"

"Oh, nothing, everything."

Then one time, coming back from the country, when Jaimie started to get in next to Schultz, his father said, "No, you come back and sit with us."

"Why?"

"Just come back."

Jaimie said nothing all the way in. It got dark outside, like the end of the world.

When they got home his father said he didn't like Jaimie's being with Schultz all the time and if it didn't stop he'd have to let Schultz go, that from then on Jaimie was to sit in the back of the car.

"Even when I'm alone with him!?"

Jaimie was so upset that his mother made his father change it: he was to sit in the back when his mother had no one else with her. That was bad enough.

Schultz was very polite to Jaimie's parents. When his father talked to Schultz through the car tube, Schultz's face never changed at all. It was funny, a man like Schultz acting, well, like a dog when he got orders. With Jaimie's mother it was not quite the same because Schultz always smiled or turned back to ask about an address.

Schultz liked Jaimie's mother because when the new car came, a Hudson landau, his mother had the front changed because she said she didn't have the heart to have a man outside in the awful Chicago weather. The car wasn't quite so elegant with the change but it was still pretty snazzy. Jaimie had never thought of his mother being like the car until once, in the late afternoon, when he and Schultz were waiting outside the dressmaker's, his mother came out in a new coat. She must have been going some place special because otherwise she never wore her sapphire necklace in the daytime. Jaimie knew that the necklace was elegant because everybody talked about it; it didn't have just blue sapphires but all colors and they were fastened together with little diamonds which, in the light, sparkled. When she came out, Schultz did a low whistle and whispered, "Elegant." Jaimie was surprised. Of course he knew that his mother was lovely. His father said so often enough and sometimes other people besides, and when he had new boyfriends at the house, afterwards they'd say, "You've a nice mother. Good-looking too."

Schultz said that women were always going into the Greek shoemakers on 47th Street. He had a curtain in the back of his shop and a little room behind it with a shoe stand.

"A shoe stand!"

"Yep. He locks the door and then later, from the little room, he lets them out in the alley."

"Why a shoe stand?"

"Lots of women like what he does better."

"What?"

Schultz slowly licked his lips.

Jaimie's mother said it was because Bessie was Irish that she was so gifted at potato peeling. She used a very sharp knife, peeled them paper thin and, when she set her mind to it, she could peel without breaking a paring. By putting eyes in them, when Jaimie was little, she used to make snakes.

"You're getting too big for the pantry now," said Bessie, who had asked him in. "Maybe that's why you like to be with Schultz so much."

Bessie was jealous!

"How come you're everybody's favorite, Jaimie?"

"Am I?"

She brought him the frosting bowl. The chocolate was not quite hard, just the way he liked it. He was her favorite, that was for sure.

On Monday nights Jaimie's father and mother had season tickets for the opera and his mother had a season ticket for the symphony on Friday afternoons. She said the real music lovers went on Saturday nights but Friday was more convenient besides being a kind of ladies' day for the nicest women in Chicago. Monday was the most fashionable night for the opera too.

On Mondays Jaimie's father and mother usually had dinner earlier and then got dressed up; Bessie wouldn't have time to eat because she had to hurry upstairs to help. After they'd gone, she'd gobble her dinner and then rush back up to Jaimie. She could be with him on other nights too, but Monday was special because of their coming home so late on account of the opera. Even so it was scary reading the sex books that Bessie had found on the shelf in the closet.

Her favorite was *The Blindness of Virtue*. It was a play about a man who was engaged to a girl and went to visit in her house. One night her parents were called away and she became frightened or cold or lonesome or something and came in his room and got in bed with him. He jumped up and ran around the room hitting the furniture and grinding his teeth and pulling his hair and saying things like, "O God, I can't stand it," "Lord help me why am I such a beast" and "Please, God, pity her." Bessie always read it aloud and got excited and red in the face but Jaimie thought it was funny.

When Jaimie told Schultz about it he said Jaimie knew too much for that kind of kid stuff.

Schultz let Jaimie steer, at first in the country and then in the city. Jaimie would sit real close with Schultz's gloved hands around him. If anything came along, Schultz would grab the wheel.

"Why did you wait so long?"

"Don't worry. I'm here."

Later he almost never grabbed the wheel no matter what happened.

"Why?"

"You've got to learn your own control."

Still he was there.

That winter they went to Coronado Beach. Jaimie and his mother took the train, Schultz drove the car out and his father came for Christmas. Jaimie wanted to drive out with Schultz but he wasn't allowed to.

At Coronado Beach there was a long esplanade with very few cars, so Schultz really taught Jaimie to drive. It wasn't very hard as Jaimie was already a good steerer. At first he sat between Schultz's legs. The only difficult part was the gas and spark lever but Schultz said they weren't important, the important thing was the brake: you've always got to have her under control, even if it's slippery and wet and then you shouldn't use the brake at all! When it rained he showed Jaimie by skidding all over the place and around to a dead stop by the water.

When Jaimie's father came out they drove down the esplanade to show him. When they reached a safe place, Schultz as usual got out to open the door, but when his father got in front beside Jaimie, Schultz didn't get back in but shut both doors. He said, "I'll wait here."

That was the only time Jaimie's father wanted Schultz next to Jaimie because he jumped out and put Schultz back in front. Jaimie drove down the esplanade, turned around and back to the starting place. But Schultz said, "Drive your father back to the hotel."

So Jaimie did. His father, who couldn't drive, was so impressed that Jaimie didn't care if he sat in front with Schultz or not . . . for a while, anyway.

That summer Jaimie's parents rented a big house in Winnetka. It was so big that besides Bessie and the cook they had to have a second maid.

Her name was Rosa. She wore glasses and came from Luxemburg and didn't smile even when she arranged the flowers.

Schultz said she was after him, that she kept bothering him and that she'd better leave him alone.

"Why?"

"She better had, that's all." Schultz was very angry. His face hardened and the sides almost twitched.

"Why, what would you do?"

"I'd give it to her until she'd wish she'd never seen me. that's what I'd do."

Schultz lived with a woman who worked nights mostly.

"Oh."

Yes, but not before fixing him up. She cooked for him wonderful and that wasn't all. He didn't run around, he didn't have to: what he got was so good.

"Is she nice?"

"Mm. hm."

"Like my mother?"

"Sweeter."

"Is she as pretty?"

"Well, she hasn't got pearls to show herself off in." Schultz laughed. "What she's got's better."

"Diamonds?"

"Yes."

"Did you give them to her?"

"God did. Here and here," and Schultz touched his chest and crotch. "I just keep 'em polished."

Schultz lived in a big block of flats on the West Side. Sometimes he drove Jaimie by but he'd never take him up.

He said there was a tall woman across the hall, red haired, a good-looker. She would come out with her negligee half open and it wasn't hard to see what she was after. But Schultz never went in.

"Why?"

"Never shit on your own doorstep, Jaimie."

Once Jaimie said, "Why don't you take me with you?"

"Where?"

"To watch."

Schultz was surprised and shocked and pleased too. He maybe thought he had a good pupil. Maybe he was tempted too because it took him a long time to say, "No."

"Why?"

"I couldn't."

Maybe he didn't dare. Jaimie kept pestering him and he always laughed as if he liked the idea until once he said, "What's the good in watching? The fun's in doing it, but what's your hurry? You'll do it fine. Half of it's making them want it, you know, and they'll want it from you."

"Why will they?"

"I see the girls look at you. They're not just looking at me up here."

Jaimie laughed but he didn't really believe that they were looking at him when they could see Schultz sitting there.

Maybe Schultz would have taken him anyway but then one morning he wasn't there.

Jaimie's father telephoned his flat but there was no answer. Then he telephoned the garage and they said the car hadn't been there all night. Yes, they were sure.

Jaimie's father was so excited that he woke up his mother. The worst part was that she got dressed and took Jaimie to school in a taxi. On the way Jaimie was so despondent that his mother said he didn't have to stay for woodcraft and could come home early. She promised to telephone him if she found out anything special.

When he came home his mother said there had been an accident. "No, not serious . . . he hurt his toe."

"His toe! Where is he?"

"In the hospital."

Jaimie wanted to go right away but his mother didn't know which hospital. His mother was not a good liar because when she did her eyes opened very wide. She didn't give a decent answer to any question and then she said what she always said when she didn't know what to say: "Wait until your father comes home."

But his father didn't tell him anything either. They both knew too. Bessie said they did. She brought him his supper like always when he didn't go downstairs and then sat and spoon-fed him the way she did when he was small. He didn't care enough to turn his head away to make her coax him.

She said she'd listened while they talked on the phone. It was about Schultz's woman, who'd been in trouble before. She had a police record.

"Did you know he lived with a woman, Jaimie?"

"Yes, I did."

"They found the car in Detroit. So it looks like they've gone over into Canada. Your mother's tortoise case with the cards and dollar bills was still there. So he wasn't a thief anyway. Maybe he murdered somebody though. But even if he did, he'll be coming back to see you anyway."

"Why will he?"

"Because you're his friend. Whenever he came into the kitchen for a snack and coffee, he'd always say, 'Hurry, please, my friend Jaimie's out there and I can't keep my best friend waiting'."

Tears trickled out.

"Your father was real nice, though. He told the police that now they'd found the car and it wasn't damaged, he was no longer interested, they didn't have to look for him."

"Oh."

"So it isn't that terrible, is it, Jaimie-boy?"

"Yes, it is, Bessie."

He turned his head away. He could understand Schultz's having taken the car, as awful as that was, but not without telling him first. Why, after all their secret talks?

Bessie took the tray and closed the door. Then, as usual, she stood outside listening. She wouldn't hear him crying though, because he'd stuffed his head in the pillow.

Jaimie told his mother that after school he was going over to Phelps Malloy's. His mother kissed him. She was happy because when Schultz was there his mother and father were always asking why he didn't go over and play with the other boys.

He took the number 4 streetcar. He sat quiet but he was not quiet inside. He didn't think Schultz was back but he wanted to see.

He didn't know the name of the street but he found the block of flats. There were so many of them he didn't know which exactly. One of them was marked JANITOR but nobody answered.

It began to rain and so he ran up and down the stairways. They were all dark and only a few of them were clean. He guessed Schultz would have lived in a clean one. All of them, though, had writing on the walls.

A tall woman with reddish hair came down the stairs. But not in a negligee.

"Excuse me. Do you know someone named Schultz?"

"Who?"

"The man who lives across the hall."

"No one lives across from me, sonny."

She put her umbrella up and went out.

He had to wait a long time for number 4 and got wet through. Riding in it was like the time in the car, cold and dark outside like the end of the world, only this time it was the end for sure.

When he got home his mother said, "Jaimie! Where have you been?"

He sneezed.

"Get those clothes off."

She came upstairs with him and ran the bath.

"Why didn't you call up? The car's back. We have another driver."

"What's he like?"

"He seems all right. He's not like Schultz, though."

He believed her.

Jaimie had caught cold. His legs ached, he had a pain on his left side and a little temperature.

The cold went away but the aches and pains stayed on and so did the temperature. Dr. Abt came, joked, tapped and listened. He said Jaimie had a touch of rheumatic fever, that it wasn't anything serious but it seemed to have affected his heart, just a little bit. He was supposed to stay in bed and rest.

"For how long?"

Well, Dr. Abt didn't know.

Afterwards there was the usual hushhush in the den with Jaimie's mother. Then Dr. Abt came back, sat on the bed and asked if Jaimie had any questions.

"Will I die?"

"I hope so — in a hundred years or maybe less. But your mother will if you worry her. Be a good boy and stay quiet."

Then he moved closer and took Jaimie's hand in his tough fat one. "Does anything bother you lately, Jaimie?"

"Did my mother tell you to ask me?"

"Would it be so terrible if she had?"

Jaimie thought it over. "No, because there isn't anything."

Jaimie's mother had beautiful hands that felt cool and lovely on his forehead. She didn't keep them there long because she always thought he felt hot and would get up to take his temperature. She was wonderful at straightening the pillows and making everything fresh. She said that when she was a girl she wanted to be a trained nurse but that her father wouldn't let her.

After breakfast in bed she'd always come in and stay with Jaimie, although she would leave to give orders for the house and of course she always had to go into her room to answer the telephone. She had many lady friends and her favorite, Alma Fellows, was almost lovelier than she. She would tell Jaimie what Alma and the others said, but she said they weren't as truthful as she was. She said she was an exceptionally truthful person. She thought a lie was an awful thing, not a white lie maybe which one said only on special occasions so as not to hurt someone's feelings.

"Like what?"

"Oh, if someone isn't looking well or has bought a hideous hat." She thought this was funny and laughed and so did Jaimie.

She said that she and Jaimie must always be truthful with one another and that it would be awful if Jaimie didn't tell her everything.

Jaimie giggled.

His mother asked why but she couldn't help laughing too. Then, as if she knew what he was thinking, she asked, "Do you miss Schultz?"

"Yes, some."

That same afternoon Phelps came over.

"Where'd you go that afternoon when you got sick?"

"Why?"

"Your mother thought you were at our place."

"How do you know?"

"She called up."

So she knew, or something anyway, and that was why she talked about lying. But was she lying too by pretending not to know? And why was he supposed to tell everything when all he ever heard was from Bessie and they didn't tell him anything that he really wanted to know?

The aches and pains got better but being in bed every day got worse. There was nothing worth anything with Schultz gone. The only man Jaimie saw was his father. He'd come home in the late afternoons, say hello and go lie down in the den. He could drop right off to sleep and in just a few minutes wake up refreshed. After dinner, when he didn't go out, he'd come and sit with Jaimie for a while. He'd tell about all the important matters he'd had to deal with, the advice he'd given and how he'd reorganized this and that. He didn't just reorganize in Chicago, he went to New York and Pittsburg and other places. For a little man, Jaimie's mother said, he was a wonder at reorganizing big companies.

Dr. Abt said Jaimie could start getting up. Gradually, at first only a few minutes, then more and more.

Jaimie's mother was so happy that she couldn't wait to tell his father if he called from Pittsburg. She kissed him and said, "Hearts of palm, alligator pear, French lamb chops and sherbert, I can't stand it anymore" and went off to her Thursday luncheon.

Bessie took her sweet time coming up with the tray. Then, when she came in, she was smiling funny.

"What's the matter with you?"

She took a letter from her apron. It was for his father.

"Look on the back."

Hermann Schultz 59 Winder St. Detroit Mich

"I'll bet you'd like to know what's in it."

Jaimie looked at her.

"I know."

"How?"

"Cross your heart."

Jaimie did.

"I steamed it open . . . because I knew you'd want to know. Look how neat I glued it back."

"Why didn't you let me see it?"

"He didn't say much except that he has three weeks pay coming and some vacation money. I say he should have thought of that before he took the car. The part about the vacation money is true, though; remember . . ."

"What else did he say?"

"He said he did it because his fiancee – he calls her his fiancee – was in trouble and they need a lawyer bad. He said he was desperate and could your father lend him five hundred dollars. He said he knew he'd done wrong but the car wasn't scratched and he'd worked honest for over two years."

"Did he say anything about me?"

"No, nor me neither." Bessie laughed.

"Take the tray."

"You didn't touch it."

"Please, Bessie."

She knew when not to argue.

500 dollars! Jaimie had 117 in the marble bag saved for everything: for the trip with Phelps to Starved Rock, for *The Negro Children's Fresh Air* and maybe for a dog next summer. Would his father

give it, or would he if Jaimie gave his 117? With Schultz so desperate Jaimie couldn't stand it any longer if they didn't tell him anything.

It was a surprise all right. What happened was that Bessie came in and said two men were bringing a crate upstairs. Of course when he saw it he knew right away what was in it because he'd wanted one for so long.

It was complete with records and with a card that said,
To while away the weary hours love Dad

He handled it like it might break. He played *When Irish Eyes are Smiling* for Bessie and because his mother asked to hear Geraldine Farrer he played *Butterfly* for her. The vic had a beautiful deep clear tone. Then he closed it and locked it.

"What are you doing that for?"

"I think Dad should take it back."

"Why?"

"He didn't know I was getting up when he sent it."

"That's the silliest thing I ever heard of."

"I'll wait and see what he thinks anyway."

"You mean you're not going to play it until Sunday!" His mother was getting mad.

"I didn't have it while I was sick, so what'll a couple more days hurt?"

His mother got up and walked out. Later she sent Bessie in to see what she could do.

"Your mother's real upset that you're so pig-headed. I must say that with that beautiful machine I don't understand it either."

It was funny that she didn't.

Would his father send the 500? Or would he if Jaimie returned the vic and gave the money-bag-money? 500 — 117 = 373. But even with the records it didn't cost that much. Worse still: if he wasn't supposed to know what was in his father's letter, how could he talk about it?

There was one chance:

"There's a letter from Schultz in the den."

"For me?"

"No, for father."

"How do you know about it?"

"I saw it. Could you read it to me? Please."

"Open someone else's mail? I wouldn't dream of such a thing."

So that was that. Maybe he'd have to tell on Bessie. He couldn't say he steamed the letter open himself because then his father might be so angry that he wouldn't send anything at all. Jaimie thought and figured and worried about it all the time. And then, like Aladdin's lamp, out of the blue, the answer came! Schultz had written him too. Jaimie wished he really had. He pretended that he had:

> Dear Jaimie,
> How are you? I miss you very much.
> Then just exactly like the letter to his
> father but with a different end:
> Much love Schultz.

Well, maybe not "much", maybe not even "love". Maybe just "your best friend Schultz."

Jaimie's mother could usually get his father to do what she wanted. Once, though, when she had asked something in front of Alma Fellows, his father had said "No" and when he left the room Alma laughed her lovely tinkly laugh and said, "Edith, you're so naive. If you really want something from Edgar, ask it lying down."

Jaimie of course knew what Alma meant but he thought it might be better if he talked with his father lying down anyway. So he did his time up early Sunday morning and was back in bed when his father came home. His father came up to see him straightaway; he was glad that Jaimie was better but he was so excited about the wonderful reorganization he'd made in Pittsburg that he couldn't wait to tell Jaimie's mother about it. First, though, he asked Jaimie how he liked the victrola but he didn't stay to hear.

His father had to tell his partner too about the wonderful reorganization and so he went out and came back late for Sunday dinner and with one thing and another he didn't come in to sit with Jaimie until Sunday afternoon.

"Well, now. Your mother tells me you've been waiting for me. You didn't have to do that, Jaimie. Let's play it."

But Jaimie didn't.

"What's the matter?"

"How much did it cost?"

"That's a strange question. Why?"

"Wouldn't it be better maybe to give the money to somebody poor?"

"We give generously enough to the poor."

"I don't mean like that. I mean somebody we know."

"Who?"

Jaimie looked down. "Schultz." When he looked up his father was staring at him.

"Did you open my letter?"

"He wrote me too."

"I'd like to see it."

"All he said was that he was sorry he took the car but his girl was in trouble and he needed five hundred dollars. Will you send it to him?"

Because Jaimie's father was still staring at him Jaimie felt he had to say more. "He said he was writing me because I was his friend and maybe I should speak with you about it."

"I see."

"Will you send it?"

"No."

"Why?"

"As a reward for stealing or to help him get mixed up with a woman of that kind?"

"How do you know what she's like?"

"She has a police record. Of course, strictly speaking that's not my concern. But what is my concern and inexcusable is for a man to involve a thirteen year old boy in his private affairs. Because of your loyalty I might have sent him something in addition to his claim, but certainly not now, for what he's done is unpardonable."

"Oh." Then very low Jaimie said, "He didn't write me."

"Then you read my letter after all?"

"Yes."

His father stood up. Jaimie thought he was going to hit him. He did worse. "You know what Schultz thinks I owe him. Well, I know of no law that states that one is obliged to pay a thief. In view of what you've done and so that you will think twice before doing such a thing again, I shall send nothing."

Jaimie lay there. Maybe he should have said how Bessie opened the letter. Maybe for Schultz's sake he should have. But even for Schultz he just couldn't tell on poor Bessie. It was her night off so his mother brought up the tray. She said his father was very upset and that Jaimie should apologize. But his father didn't come in again.

Jaimie took down the marble bag. There was 90 in bills and 27 in change. He stuffed in handkerchiefs so the coins couldn't rattle and put the bag in his mackintosh. It would look funny traveling without a suitcase and so he took his schoolbag. He put in the cold meat from the tray and a sweater and scarf to stuff it out with.

Downstairs everything was like always before he'd been sick: the umbrella stand, the front parlour, the dent in the wall near the washroom. He opened the vestibule door and closed it until he heard the click. Then he put his shoes on. It was cold and so he tied the scarf around his head. He wasn't shaky at all.

In the streetcar it wasn't like the time he'd gone to Schultz's flat because then he knew he shouldn't have gone. This time he had to go; because Schultz wasn't getting any money at all just on account of something Jaimie had done; why, Schultz didn't even know about it! Jaimie hoped that the 117 less the train fare would be as much as the salary anyway.

It was still dark in Detroit. Although the money was for Schultz Jaimie took a taxi because he felt wobbly and besides it would have been dangerous scrounging around a strange city with so much money.

59 Winder St. had a vacancy sign in the window. Even so Jaimie had to ring twice before a woman came to the door. She said, "Oh, number 14 on the top floor." As Jaimie started up a bell rang.

Climbing the stairs Jaimie had to rest twice and when he got to the top he was all in. Schultz, bare-chested and bare-footed, was coming out of a room rubbing his eyes like he just woke up. He looked awful: he hadn't shaved and his eyes were puffed. He was so surprised to see Jaimie that he didn't smile. Then he said, "Jaimie, you're so white."

"I've been sick. Can I sit down?"

"Sit here." Schultz pulled down a seat attached to the wall under a telephone. Jaimie thought of their old talks about Schultz's girl and guessed that maybe if he was dying Schultz wouldn't invite him in.

"Why'd you come?"

"Here." Jaimie took out the bag. "It's a hundred and seventeen dollars less . . . well, it's more than a hundred anyway. My father won't send anything."

"Where'd you get this?"

"It's mine. Can I have some water?"

Schultz took the bag and went back in the room. A woman's voice said, "Who?" and then excitedly, "What?!" There was a lot of talking and walking around. Then the door opened and the woman said, "Don't take it there, bring him here" and Schultz came out, this time with his shoes on. He helped Jaimie up and steered him towards the room.

When they got to the door the woman was there. She was in a blue wrapper with a slip underneath that was tight across her big breasts. She was very blond and although not so young very pretty with wonderful white skin that was powdered and smelled lovely even before Jaimie got in the room.

"Hello, honey," she said, and then to Schultz, "Why don't you help him, you big lummox?" and she came out and put her arms under Jaimie's. "I didn't know you were such a big fellow . . . and so good-looking too. You must be dog-tired, all that way with all that money."

They were in the room and her perfume was stronger, some kind of Arabian flowers maybe with lilies of the valley.

"Aren't you the wonder boy! A friend in need is a friend indeed. I could kiss you for it. I think I will."

She did everything at once, very quick, talking all the time: helped him down, gave him water, closed the window, opened his tie, put him back on the pillow. As she bent down, he could see in the cleft between her great breasts where Schultz had said the diamonds were and her perfume was so sweet and strong that he forgot everything else.

"You're not going to faint, are you?"

He shook his head.

"Well, don't. Anna'll take care of you. I should after all you've done for us. You've saved us. You're our little gentleman saviour. But wait, I'll get you something better than water."

There was a wash basin and next to it a gas burner on the bureau. She filled a kettle and put it on. "Is there a drop of rum?" and when

24

Schultz showed her the empty bottle, she said, "Go down and get some ... Old Jamaica ... we can afford it for him."

It was the first time Jaimie had ever been glad to see Schultz leave. It was so funny that he couldn't help smiling: because he had always wanted to come to their flat in Chicago and Schultz wouldn't take him and here in Detroit right off he was in their bed!

Anna took his shoes off, loosened his belt, pulled his trousers off, covered him. She put her hand on his forehead, like his mother but different, not so cool and soothing, but better as if her hand was there to stay. No one had ever touched him like that before.

"My, you're pale. Are you all right?"

He nodded and Schultz came back. Anna took a piece of cake from the box by the window, poured the tea – two cups full – put rum in it and then sat on the bed and spooned it to him. He didn't like it alone but with the crumbly old cake it was just wonderful.

He could hear Schultz blowing and sipping but he couldn't see him. Then Schultz stopped and asked, "Did anyone know you were going away?"

Jaimie shook his head.

"They'll know you've gone though, won't they?"

"What time is it?"

"Nine."

"Maybe."

Anna went on spooning the tea. It was hard to keep his eyes open. As they went shut he saw the white of her lovely skin.

"They'll know you're here, won't they?"

"I guess so."

"I don't like it that they haven't phoned."

"Why?" Anna asked. "Here, honey, finish it and then you can sleep."

"Because I know Jaimie's dad and he won't fool around. If he doesn't find this number he'll call the police."

"Oh!" Anna said and stopped spooning the tea. Jaimie opened his eyes. "Maybe you ought to call him, Hermann."

"Why?" Jaimie asked. "Can't I stay with you a little first? Please."

"Maybe Hermann can tell him you're tuckered out and should rest up with us for a while. We want you, honey. But go on, Hermann, before it's too late."

Jaimie was going to say something but Anna kissed him again. "Take it easy," Schultz said, "He's just thirteen and we've had enough trouble." Then he went out.

"You don't like the police much," Jaimie said when the door closed.

"They don't like me, honey."

"Why?"

"I got into trouble, like Hermann said."

"How?"

"I did something wrong."

Jaimie smiled. "It couldn't have been so bad."

"Why?" She smiled back.

"Because you're so nice."

She kissed him again. "It wasn't so nice to pinch your daddy's car. Still and all, bygones are bygones, and it couldn't be helped. What's bad about it is that now we need help with the law and after what's happened we can't turn to your dad. Hermann says he's such a wonderful lawyer he could get anybody out of anything. Do you believe that? Hermann said he's not so hot at home though and no good with you at all. Why? What does he do to you, honey?"

"Nothing. I don't see him much."

"Maybe you're lucky. They're all alike, rich or poor. You should have seen mine . . . what a stinker. He never gave me nothing decent. Come to think of it, you're the only man who ever gave me money for nothing and that's the truth. I'll never forget it. Never."

He heard it far off and smiled. He didn't want her to forget . . . . . .

"Wake up, honey. I'm sorry you're so sleepy but you can sleep later. You gotta get up now. Look, here's a bacon and egg sandwich all hot and milk. Eat it, honey, and then you gotta go back with Hermann."

"Why do I?"

"Because that's what your daddy said."

"When?"

"An hour or so ago." It was Schultz behind her in the corner. She was dressed now in green, with green lace at her breasts and on her sleeves. She still smelled wonderful.

"Your father said you'd been real sick and that your mother's worried about drafts and everything and that you might get heart trouble again . . . So I rented a car with a heater. A Macfarland, Jaimie, the kind you always wanted. It's down in front. You can help me drive her back."

"Are you going?"

She shook her head.

"Then I won't go."

"It's not such a bad idea at that," Schultz said. "We don't have to stay overnight, so who'll know . . . except Jaimie's folks. And if you take care of Jaimie on the way, his father might want to thank you, Anna. Yes, I think his folks would appreciate it."

"Oh, I'd do it just for him."

"Then will you go?" Jaimie asked.

"Yes, for you."

"I'll go for you too."

Jaimie slept all the way to South Chicago. When he woke up his head was in Anna's lap with the flaps of her fur coat around him and she'd covered his feet with a blanket. She'd been dozing too and when he moved she opened her eyes and smiled. She had a red and green handkerchief around her head and with the fur at her neck she looked prettier than ever. As Jaimie sat up he kissed her on the cheek.

"Hey, hey," Schultz said. He must have seen them in the mirror.

Jaimie had to get out and when Schultz pulled up he saw the sky. As he stood in the back of the car he could see the fires from the mills in a great line along the lake. With the red sky in the cold air they were like suns or volcanos maybe with the fires coming from inside the earth. It was strange and so beautiful, so different from what he had known of Chicago that it was hard to believe that the mills at night were really part of it, just as it was hard to believe that a person like Anna was part of a world so near and yet a world that he had never known.

When he got back in the car, Schultz said, "Aren't you going to spell me? You're a fine pal; you don't help me drive and you take my girl." Then he drove off and the red faded outside and it was black again broken every once in a while by the first city lights.

Jaimie said nothing. He was dreaming how he'd like to go over the whole world with Schultz driving and Anna so warm next to him seeing mills at night and other wonders that he didn't know.

"What are you thinking, honey?"

"About the mills . . . how beautiful they made everything far away."

"They don't make things so beautiful near up," Anna said. "I know."

The lights were all on in the house. Schultz got out but Anna sat there and so did Jaimie.

"Are you scared of your folks?"

Jaimie shook his head. "I just wanted to stay with you a little more." Then he got out but Anna didn't.

"Aren't you coming?" Schultz asked.

"I don't know," she said, so Jaimie decided it. "Come on," he said and took her by the hand. He was still holding her hand when his father opened the door.

"Oh, so it's you." His father didn't kiss him or pat him or anything. He just looked at him real mean and then, almost friendly-like, said hello to Schultz.

"Jaimie!" his mother called from the top of the stairs. She was waiting for him to come up but he didn't move. It was lucky he hadn't because with his father staring at him like that he suddenly felt dizzy and grabbed the bannister. He sat on the bottom step and couldn't see his mother dabbing her eyes as she came down the stairs but he heard her. "Oh how could you do such a thing to me?" and then, next to him, her voice changed. "Jaimie, what is it?! You're not ill again?"

"He's just exhausted, Madame," Schultz said. "He was pale like that in Detroit."

"Well, help me, someone, get him to bed."

Jaimie's father hadn't moved but Schultz had. He picked Jaimie up and started up the stairs. Over Schultz's shoulder he saw Anna and wanted to say "Come up with us" but he was done in this time for sure and so he just smiled. Anna smiled back and called "Be careful, honey." His mother was so surprised that she missed a step and rolled her eyes.

Schultz put him on the bed and started to unlace his shoes.

"I can do the rest, Schultz," his mother said. "Jaimie's father is waiting to talk to you and he'll thank you, I'm sure, far better than I can."

She helped him undress and into his pyjamas. She said he was as white as a sheet and she kept asking how he felt, if she shouldn't call Dr. Abt even though it was so late, if he didn't want her to wake Bessie to heat him up something hot. Jaimie said no, he was all right, he was just tired, but it wasn't true. His side had begun to hurt again.

"Go to sleep then, dear." She kissed him and went to the door. "Is there anything else you'd like?"

"I'd like to see Anna."

His mother stopped dead. "She must be with Schultz talking to your father. And it's so late . . . it's after one." And as if two reasons weren't enough, "Do you know what sort of woman she is?"

"Yes."

"Then . . . I'd really like to know . . . what do you like about her?"

"Everything."

Jaimie lay there. He dozed off and then he thought he heard footsteps in the hall and Anna say, "Oh sir, I can't thank you enough." The voices were going down the stairs when she said, "But I don't like to go without telling Jaimie goodbye" and his mother said, "I'll tell him for you . . . It's out of the question. You forget that he's still very very young."

Jaimie jumped up. His side really hurt so that he had to stop before going on. The outside door closed, the motor turned over and the car drove away. When he reached the hall, the lights switched off downstairs and his mother started up.

"Jaimie, what are you doing?"

"Where are they?"

"Did you think they were spending the night?" His father was coming up after her. "Go to bed."

"What happened?"

"What do you think happened?" Whatever it was, it must have been bad because his father was so angry. "I paid ransom, just as if you'd been kidnapped. Isn't that what you wanted all along?"

"You don't have to yell, Edgar."

"I have to yell to get some sense in him. If he's so fond of these people, he should know what they are."

"Your father's right, Jaimie. Money was all they cared about. Why, after they got it, they didn't give a second thought to you or . . ."

"That's not true. Anna asked to say goodbye to me."

"Are you calling your mother a liar?"

"I heard her."

"Well, you won't hear her again. Because the condition I made was on the understanding that they won't ever come back to – "

"Jaimie! Oh God, Edgar, call Dr. Abt."

Bessie was putting something on his tongue. The pain wasn't so bad now. The light in the corner was shaded with a towel or something. Bessie patted him and said, "Dr. Abt will be here any minute now. So don't worry, Jaimie-boy."

He wasn't worried if Dr. Abt came or not or what he'd say this time about would he die or not. He didn't care because how could he ever find Anna again, and drink bitter tea, and hear what was real from Schultz, and see the night all red, and smell her perfume when she touched him and called him honey?

Poor Hubert

Hubert had the funeral meats stacked and ready. All Len and I had to do was to carry them to the car. We put the boxes on the back seat and the bottles with the coffee container on the floor and drove off.

"Who was the beautiful woman, Len, whom you and Hubert kissed?"

"How could you see her through that veil?"

"Why was she in mourning?"

"Her father died." Len smiled. Although he wasn't any longer a boy he hadn't really changed. He had the same jet black hair and black eyes and the same sweet shy smile.

We drove out through Jackson.

"It was a funny funeral . . . those men in caps and aprons."

"It was what your grandfather wanted," Len said. "He was a 32 degree mason, wasn't he? Well, the music was beautiful anyway."

"Hubert's a wonder."

"You always liked dad. Do you say it now on account of the music?"

"On account of everything. As if arranging the funeral wasn't enough. At the last minute mother gets the idea that because it's a beautiful day instead of going to your house it would be nicer at the lake, and without a word he rushes home and packs up everything."

"He thought it was a nice idea too. Don't you?"

"Sure, but he does all the work."

"It's the right place, after all the summers your family have spent at the cottage, in memory of Uncle Jake. When do you think he built the cottage?"

"Oh, fifty years ago, I guess."

We turned off the main road and took the road to the lake. It had been macadamized; the improvement broke the charm. When it was

31

a dirt road, the woods had seemed wilder and probably were. In the old days, mother always complained about the dust, and if she was in the swing and saw a cloud from an approaching car, she'd run into the cottage, wrinkling up her nose. Not that there were many cars. There were none now for the season was over. We pulled up in back of the cottage and below through the trees was the lake. There was hardly a ripple. Across, toward the station end, there were two fishing boats.

"It's a long time since you've been here, Jaimie."

"Do you still come every year, Len?"

"I always came out from Jackson to see Uncle Jake, but it was never the same without you here. Your love for it shed on me. But then, when I was a little boy, I thought everything you thought. You knew everything about it, the paths, the lake, where the turtles were, the bogs that were safe when we went frogging. I remember everything you told me. How to tell the poison ivy and the poison sumac, and about the snakes, how to watch out for them in August, when they shed and were blind. You were patient with me, Jaimie."

"You were like a little brother for the summer, the only one I ever had. In my room at home I used to mark the days off on a calendar before coming here. This place was everything . . . freedom and being with the family, you, Gramps, Aunt Florence and my parents, for that matter, when they were here."

"But you had them at home too, Jaimie."

"Not really. They were always occupied with being important. I was never really with them. I was with the servants. You never had that. We'd better unload the car."

The cottage had not been closed for the winter but the curtains were down around the porch and hooked to the screens. We rolled them up, unpacked the food, uncorked the wine and set the table. I took a pitcher and went down to the well. Going down the steps I remembered the fussing in the old days, before the cottage had running water, about who should get it. When old Tante Regina, Len's grandmother, was visiting us, she would get up at five to putter around the kitchen. As there was never enough water from the night before, she would go to the well for it and afterwards there were always family discussions about how it was a disgrace to let her carry it, that something should be done, but nothing was done.

I had started out on the dock when I heard voices from the cottage. The family had arrived.

No one had cried at the funeral but as we sat down around the table Tina began. She had not been well, and the ceremony and then the cemetery and the ride to the lake had been too much for her. "Oh Uncle Jake," she wailed, "When I think of all he did for us."

Aunt Florence, the biggest and softest in the family and the kindest too, hadn't cried at all but Tina started her off. Florence's crying encouraged Tina's.

"To think how he brought mamma and me over and took care of us through the years. And I was just a baby." The thought of her babyhood was so heart-breaking that Tina sobbed aloud.

"There, there," Hubert said, patting her. "Everyone knows the story."

Boo hoo from Aunt Florence. Uncle Sol blew his nose, a great blast.

"He was like a father to me," Tina sobbed. "He loved me so."

This was too much for my mother. As the only child of my grandfather's first marriage she had always assumed first place in his affections and now Tina and Florence were stealing the show. She began to cry too.

"For God's sake, Edith," my father said. "He had a full life. He was a hundred and three years old."

"I don't care," said my mother, who had made up her mind to cry.

The weeping, with Sol's blowing, made quite a quartet. The rest of us looked at each other and smiled.

"Every month, as long as mamma lived, no matter what happened, he gave me a cheque," Tina went on. "Even after that, from Florida, he always sent . . ."

"Tina!" Hubert cautioned. But it was too late.

"He did!" Uncle Arthur said. "For how much? You kept his books, Sol. Why didn't you ever tell us?"

"I never knew it."

"How could you not know it? You saw his stubs."

"There was never anything for Tina. There were cheques to Hubert, for repairs on the cottage, but nothing regular. Why did you say there were, Tina?"

Tina didn't know what to say. She looked at Hubert. He didn't know what to say either.

"Maybe he had a private account," my father said. He thought this was funny.

"Come to think of it," Arthur said, "For years he had a cheque-book on a Detroit bank. He'd never let me see it. He said he never used it, that it was in case of emergencies."

"He sent you cheques each month all those years in Florida!" my mother said. "Why? I could have understood it when you and Hubert were first married, and when Leonard was born, when you needed it, but . . ."

"Why don't you tell them, dad?" Len said.

"Uncle Jake never wanted anyone to know."

"What difference does it make now?"

"The cheques weren't to Tina," Hubert said. "They were to me for Marjorie."

"Marjorie!"

"Who was Marjorie?"

"Ida Towitt's daughter," Tina said hopefully, as if it could explain everything.

"Ida Towitt, Ed's wife?" Sol asked.

"She used to come to see mother," Florence said, her voice trembling.

"I never liked her," my mother said.

"She and Ed had separated," Hubert said. "Uncle Jake made an arrangement with him. Marjorie took his name."

"When did this happen?" my father, always the great lawyer, asked.

"After Mother L died."

"He was over seventy," said my father, who was sixty-nine.

"Seventy-five," Hubert said. "After she died, he was very lonesome. You'd all gone away except for the summers here at the lake. Ida kept him company. I guess she was lonesome too."

"I'm glad he had someone after mother died," Florence said.

"You mean you're glad it happened!" Arthur said.

"I don't think it happened at all," my mother said.

"Why not, Edith?" my father asked.

"Father was always such a respected man. And at that age." She seemed to look at my father. "There's really no proof anyway, is there,

34

Hubert?"

"There's no proof that you're his daughter either, mother."

"What a terrible thing to say."

"Tell us about her," Florence said, her voice still trembling. "Did father ever see her?"

"He used to at our house," Tina said. "He adored her. We all did. She was an exceptionally lovable little girl."

"And so pretty," Len said.

"How do you know?" my father asked.

"I used to play with her."

"I think that's terrible," my mother said.

"What is?" I asked.

"Everything. Why didn't you tell us, Tina?"

"Uncle Jake asked us not to."

"What happened to her?" I asked.

"When Ida died, Uncle Jake sent her to school in Switzerland. She wanted to learn languages. She studied singing. She was always very musical. She has a lovely voice."

"We thought she'd become an opera singer," Tina said.

"She wanted to," Hubert went on. "But a man from Grand Rapids met her there. He fell in love with her and when she came home she married him."

"Did Gramps give her away?"

"Jaimie, I don't think that's funny."

"Well, she was his child."

The bare fact shocked the legitimates.

"Her husband died last year," Hubert said. "He was much older than she was."

"What does she do?" mother asked.

"She's active musically in Grand Rapids and in Detroit too. Sometimes she sings professionally."

"Can she support herself that way?"

"She doesn't have to, Edith. Her husband was a very rich man."

This somehow shocked mother more. "Did she know father was her father?"

"She called him Uncle Jake but, yes, of course she did. She was very fond of him. She came to see him every year."

"Where?"

35

"Here, at the lake. When you were all away, she'd drive down from Grand Rapids."

"Wasn't father cunning?" Arthur said.

"Pour the coffee, Edith," my father said. No one had touched the food.

"I don't want to pour the coffee. I think its very disloyal of you and Hubert, Tina. After all that father's done for you and we have too. It's so ungrateful."

"What could you have done about it, sis?" Arthur asked.

"It's not a question of what we could have done. It was our right to know."

"It wasn't our right to tell, Edith," Tina said, "When Uncle Jake didn't want us to. Our first loyalty was to him."

"That seems quite clear," my mother said and stood up. "I'm going home. This place and everything else has been spoiled for me." She started out and stopped. "I suppose father left it to Marjorie."

"No, he didn't," Hubert said. "He took care of her years ago."

"How?" Arthur asked. "For how much, do you know?"

"I can only imagine what it must be now," Hubert said. "He did it when she was born."

"Uncle Jake took care of everyone," Tina said happily.

"You know a great deal more about father's affairs than we, his own children, do."

"Obviously, Edith, in this case he went to Hubert just because Hubert wasn't his child," my father said.

"He seems to have gone to Hubert for everything else too."

My father laughed. "All of you have always asked Hubert to take care of everything for him, here at the cottage and in Jackson as well. Hubert even made all the arrangements for the funeral, which is more than what you call his own children did."

"That's absurd, Edgar," my mother said. "Hubert's in Jackson."

"There's no law that I know of that says one of you couldn't have come to Jackson to help him. He even thought of the music. You yourself said it was so beautiful, Edith. It's you who are ungrateful."

"I'm sorry, Hubert. Forgive me, Tina," and she kissed her. "I'm just so upset." She put her hand on Hubert's arm. "The music was really lovely. The organist and the singer . . . how you ever found them in Jackson, I don't know. It was a wonderful idea, thank you."

"It wasn't mine, Edith. It was Marjorie's." Mother withdrew her hand. "She brought them from Detroit. She wanted something beautiful for her father."

"I'd like to meet Marjorie sometime," Florence said. "Well, if you're going, Edith, I'll go with you."

"We'll all go," Arthur said.

"Before next summer, Hubert," mother said, "The screens should all be changed. And the boathouse . . ."

"You don't have to do this now, Edith," my father said." You can phone Hubert from Chicago."

"Will you lock up, Hubert?" Arthur said and started out.

"I'll lock up," I said.

"Why?" mother asked. "Aren't you coming with us?"

"I'd like to stay a little while. I haven't been here for so long."

"I'd like to stay with you," Len said.

"You never want to come when we're here, Jaimie," my father said, taking a sandwich. "Well, there should be enough to eat to last you."

"If there's a storm coming," Hubert said, laughing as he went out, "Don't you boys take the boat around the point."

The canoe was water-tight. When they shoved off after supper that evening the lake was as smooth as glass. There was no breeze, the lull before the storm except it looked as if the storm had passed with lightning over the Hogsback. Gramps thought it had. Not that he knew what they were up to. Len put up the sail. It was a toy sail really, for fun. Sometimes though, if there was a little breeze, it took them a ways. As long as they stayed near the shore they were allowed to paddle where they wanted on their end of the lake, but never around the point. The water was so deep there that it was said to be bottomless. Jaimie shouldn't have promised of course; he knew the lake and how the storms came up but Len had so wanted to go and it was his last chance for the summer; Hubert was coming from Jackson that night to take Len back in the morning. When they got around the point, there was lightning in the distance beyond the foot of the lake and a heaviness in the air and then, without warning, when the storm hit them, there wasn't a chance of getting back. There wasn't a chance of going anywhere except where the blow took them and that was toward Two Tree Island.

Len looked so small. "I'll drown. I can't swim that far."

"You can float, Lennie."

"I'll drown. Let's pray, Jaimie. I'm going to pray."

"Paddle too, Len."

Len was holding on to the sides; he was too frightened to paddle but it didn't make any difference. It was the wind in the sail with Jaimie's paddle for a rudder that steered them in the cove. The canoe was filling up so fast that if they hadn't made it then it would have sunk for sure. Jaimie jumped out and pulled it in and they both pulled it up on the shore. They were only a few feet from the hut but they didn't think about Loony Bill at all. All they thought about was that they were on land and the storm.

Of course they knew about Loony Bill, everybody did. He had been in the Jackson Penitentiary because he'd killed a man. He was a thief and he fished at night and slept by day, and he ate snakes and frogs. He came to the island every spring; it was mostly swamp, nobody went there. He never came near the cottagers. Gramps knew him though. If he was fishing late near the island and saw Loony Bill he always gave him something, tobacco and bait and money too sometimes and once he gave him his rod and reel. Gramps said you should have seen his eyes. In the spring Loony Bill broke into the cottages and took tools and bedding and food if there was any but he never broke into theirs. The year the fire burnt down the Wentworth cottage they thought it was Loony Bill but it turned out he wasn't there that spring. Gramps said he was just like any other man but it was better to stay away from him.

Loony Bill was as surprised to see them as they were to see him. He had a mean-looking yellow dog that started for them. Loony Bill kicked him and said, "Get down" and then to them, "Get out." Well, which was worse, outside or in? but when they started out he said, "Wait a minute. Aren't you old Jake's boys?" and when they said they were he said "Stay then." He was a dark man, dirty and skinny, like a gypsy without a ring in his ear. He had black teeth and was smoking a corncob. There was a fire in a kind of fireplace with a pot on it and an old mattress on the floor and a broken bench and open cupboards made of planks that looked stuffed with everything that maybe he'd stolen. The walls were stopped up with papers and rags; there was no window; there was no air either. Loony Bill's feet were bare and black and his shoes were by the fire. There was a big knife in one of them.

"Snug as a bug in a rug in here, ain't it?" he said. "Any port in a storm. Well, you can't get no wetter. Before you get them clothes off, go out in back and get me some wood. The little one can stay with me."

But the little one didn't want to stay with him. He'd seen the knife and he'd sided up so close to Jaimie that Loony Bill thought it was funny. "You're right," he said to Len, "There're three things you never trust. You know what they are? Men, women and children. Women is the worst."

Instead of bringing the wood they would have run away but there was no place to run to. Then there was a burst of thunder somewhere in back of the hut.

When they came back in the dog didn't go for them again. Loony Bill put the wood near the fire. Then he said, "Get them clothes off." But he didn't wait, he helped them and the reason was that he wanted to see what was in their pockets. He took from Jaimie's a quarter, a knife, a whistle and a harmonica. "I'll keep these for you," he said, putting the whistle and quarter on a ledge, and then he went through Len's where he found another harmonica and six cents. "Not bad," he said, putting the pennies with the quarter. "Can you boys play tunes?" and when they said they could he said, "Let's hear 'em." Jaimie played mostly chords but Len could make his harmonica sing and together they were really good. Loony Bill was all black teeth with smiles. "We'll have a regular Sing Sing tea party," he said. "You know what that is? Well, you'll see" and he fished out an old tea can and put a spoonful of tea in the pot. "This is the real stuff," he said. "But that don't mean anything to you, does it? You're rich boys, ain't you?" His eyes squinted and he looked real mean.

"No," Len said and then he had an inspiration. "Jaimie was a beggar."

"Where?"

"In Chicago."

"When?"

"When he was four."

"Did you make money?"

"Yes."

"Did he take it to his folks?"

"To his cousins," Len said. "He begged with his cousins. Three girls, the littlest one danced. Her name was Jessie."

"How much did you make?"

"A lot."

Loony Bill was impressed. "I wish I'd had a kid. I'd have gone into begging and my life'd been different."

"Jaimie sang, in French too," Len said. "Sing it, Jaimie," and Len started *Parlez-moi d'Amour* and Jaimie sang it with his hand over his heart the way he used to.

"That's what I missed," Loony said. "I always wanted to learn French. Sing it again," and when Jaimie did, he said "How'd the girl dance?" and so Jaimie danced the time step the way Jessie had.

"And you got money for that!" Loony said. "Why'd you stop begging then?"

"The girls went away."

"There," Loony said to Len, banging the bench. "Didn't I tell you? Three things you never trust and the worst is women."

He poured the tea, his in a chipped cup, the boys' in a tin. He had some dirty old rock crystal candy; when they dipped it in the tea the dirt dissolved. He never let them stop playing and singing and they didn't want to because they were afraid of what might happen if they did. They sang the songs he liked over and over: *Steamboat Bill Coming Down the Mississippi* and *Mississippi Mud*. He was a little loony like his name; he thought he was Steamboat Bill and when they'd come to the refrain he'd take Jaimie's whistle and go toot toot, and when they played *Mississippi Mud* he'd get up and do the penitentiary jig. He said he liked the songs about the Mississippi best, not because he happened to have killed a man there but because he'd been happy there. He said that was why he liked to be near water. But he kept coming back to talking about begging. He was always thinking about it. He said that when you came down to it, kids can always make money. He kept saying, "What do you think? Don't you think the three of us would make a real partnership?" He got so excited about the idea that they were afraid that when the rain stopped he wouldn't let them go and they were afraid of falling asleep too because they didn't know what he would do. As it got later and Len's eyes began to close, Jaimie had to keep pinching him to keep him awake. They must have been there until after midnight when the dog got up and growled. The wind had died down and he'd heard something. Then the door opened . . . and there was Hubert!

"I wonder if your grandfather knew Loony Bill before?"
"How?"
We had taken the wine and food out on the porch. It was pleasant there, being with Len again, watching the sun go down over the lake and in the afterglow.
"Tina said he used to go to the penitentiary on Sundays. He took her once when she was a little girl. He talked to the men and organized work that they were paid for. I thought he might have known Loony there."
"That was before Loony's time, Len."
"I suppose that was how he learned to talk with convicts."
"You didn't have to learn. Remember?"
"Well, Loony was just about our mental age . . . I'll never forget when dad came in that door. I was so glad to see him I couldn't talk. I was all choked up. When he picked me up . . . he had you by the hand, I think . . . and said 'Are you all right, Len?' I just couldn't say anything. And that knife! You must have been more frightened that I was, but even I was old enough to know that he was unstable, that although he'd been friendly he could change."
"I was afraid that he wouldn't change, that he'd keep us there."
"I don't remember anything after dad came."
"He gave Loony money, everything he had, I think, and then rowed us back. He had a tarpaulin and put us under it, it was still drizzling and we towed the canoe. When we got to the cottage they had water boiling and the fire going and Gramps' old tub by it and they put us in it. You fell asleep and Hubert carried you upstairs."
"It's funny, all the talk about traumas . . . how almost drowning and being with a lunatic doesn't affect a kid at all."
"It affected me."
We drank for a while.
"For the first time that night I saw what real love was. When Hubert carried you upstairs, it was almost dawn. I went to bed but I couldn't sleep. I suppose I was over-excited. Anyway, when the cottage had quieted down, I sneaked out to the kitchen and climbed out over the rafters and looked down in your room. What I saw changed me,

without warning, from a curious boy to an outsider looking in. For you were asleep but not alone; Hubert was with you, slowly, gently, endlessly it seemed, stroking your hair. I crawled back to bed and lay there a different boy, for I'd seen what I knew I'd never have."

"And Tina always told me that you had everything, Jaimie, and I believed her. It's strange, though, isn't it, because Cousin Edith's always talking about love and she was the one who was most affected by Marjorie too."

"Mother always thought she was Gramps' favorite and Marjorie was a threat, the last one."

"Wasn't she his favorite? Tina said the great love of Uncle Jake's life was your grandmother and that when she died he transferred his love to your mother."

"I think he did. But then he had other children and Marjorie too."

"How old was Uncle Jake when he married? I think it was before he brought mother and my grandmother over."

"Oh no. It was after he brought them and Aunt Johanna too. He married late, he was almost forty. I know the story very well. Besides the store, he used to trade in wool. Every year he'd wait until the rains were over and then drive south, through southern Michigan and the border states. He loved Michigan . . . he knew every tree along the way. Anyway, that year, as he was crossing into Indiana, the rains started again and he drove into a friend's place. And there was Rachel. I think she was just seventeen. Tall, straight, very beautiful, and they fell in love. He worshipped her. It was a good marriage for her too, not only because he was so successful; the great lover and the strong father all in one, beauty and the wonderful beast. Gramps, they say, always had a way with the girls. They were married that winter. When he brought her to Jackson and drove down Main . . . she was in a sealskin coat and turban . . . didn't you ever see the photograph? . . . she was said to be the most beautiful woman in southern Michigan. Your grandmother and Aunt Johanna had the house on First made over. There was even a maid and, extravagance of extravagances, a dressing room; no one had ever heard of such a thing. She was everything he desired, or so Aunt Johanna used to say: beautiful and industrious, polite and a little distant with the relatives, courteous and shy with the callers, bending and close only for Jacob. And then the next winter the idyll was over: Rachel bore her lord the child and died."

"Tina said that he was heartbroken. He really was a lord, though, wasn't he? He was so responsible. Do you think it was her death that made him that way?"

"He was that way to begin with. He brought all his family over before he married. But maybe men were more responsible then, or some of them, and families were closer. But it wasn't just families. Look at your grandfather."

"He didn't really have the choice."

"Why? A young country doctor. He didn't have to go to all those people. Do you think it really was cholera . . . in southern Germany?"

"It could have been. Of course they didn't know so much about diseases then. If they had, perhaps he wouldn't have died. But they don't know so much about them either now, Jaimie."

Tina died that winter. I was at Medical School and mother wrote that the family had decided that it wasn't necessary to go en masse to the funeral and that Uncle Sol would represent them. When Sol returned from Jackson she was so moved by his account of Hubert's grief that she wrote to Hubert to invite him to the lake the following summer. But the strange thing is that Hubert didn't come and, stranger still, he wasn't in Jackson that summer at all. And then the next winter mother wrote that there were rumours that he had remarried. It didn't seem possible, he had been so devoted to Tina and it was so unlike him, in any case, not to have written; it probably wasn't true.

I was at home in June when Hubert and his bride called on us. In fact I opened the door.

"Why, Hubert," I said, surprised at his being there and delighted too. He looked so young and happy and almost dapper in summer flannels topped with a panama, all doubtless because of the young woman at his side, ash blond and so lovely, and definitely his or rather he was definitely hers from the fond way her hands were locked around his arm.

"Why, Hubert," I said again, grabbing him. "I'm so glad to see you. Congratulations."

"Jaimie," he said, "This is my wife. Marge, Jaimie."

"Don't I kiss the bride? . . ." and I did. "Welcome. Come in."

We came through the entrance hall, past old Louisa, who was late in answering the call, into the living room. It was an elegant room and country cousins were habitually impressed, but not Marge; her eyes were all for Hubert. "Sit next to me, darling," she said as she unlocked his arm and took his hand.

"You look wonderful, Hubert."

"I should," he said, "I've done nothing but travel."

"And see museums," she added. They both laughed.

"Shall I tell him?" he asked.

"If you want to."

"Marge said she'd always betrayed her first husband in museums. Because before Marge went away to school, she and I always used to talk about going to Europe someday and seeing everything together . . . you know, like the Winged Victory, the Last Supper and things like that. Only she saw them with her first husband . . ."

"But I always thought of Hubert."

"Isn't that nice?"

"It is now," I said and we all laughed. I asked about Len and Hubert told me that he had joined them for a while and that he was back at Ann Arbor and had decided to study medicine. "Like you, Jaimie."

"Like his grandfather."

"Do you know that your grandfather left a policy for Len's education?"

"No, but I'm not surprised. It's the least he could have done after all you did for him."

"Marge says he was the last of the patriarchs."

"He lived long enough."

"The way he founded the family . . . in the promised land . . . and took care of them."

"My mother was Hagar," Marge said and smiled.

"But you weren't Ishmael," I said. "You weren't sent into the desert. Or did you feel that you were?"

"Oh no. Coming here Hubert told me how your mother always felt that she was father's favorite child but I felt that too. He made me feel that he always loved me more than anyone else in the world."

"I'm sure he did," I said

"Hubert said he always loved you too."

"He had the gift," Hubert said.

"He had the love, darling," Marge said.

44

"Like Hubert," I said.

Marge looked at me. "When did you find out?"

"Oh long ago, ever since one night when I looked down and saw him with Len. They didn't see me. Len was asleep. After that I was always jealous of Len for having him."

"Of me?!" Hubert said.

"You were such a wonderful father."

"What about yours?" Hubert said. It wasn't so much a question as a statement, meaning mine was as good or better.

"He wasn't in your class."

"I can't believe my ears," my mother said as she came in and greeted them. She couldn't believe her eyes either as she registered Marge's youth and loveliness and appraised her handsome suit, crocodile shoes, bag and pearls. It all spelled something so different from what she had expected that her eyes widened but there was more to come, for when, by way of conversation, she asked, "What are your and Hubert's plans?" and Marge said, "I hope we have a lot of children," mother was really shocked. She covered it by ringing for Louisa to ask if tea or drinks were preferred, but neither was. Marge said that they'd come only to say hello and had to leave because she didn't like Hubert driving after dark.

We walked to the door with them. "Come and see us," Marge said to me and then the elevator came and they were gone.

"Well, I'll never get over that as long as I live," mother said. "Hubert!" and she laughed. "What did you think of her?"

"The family can be very proud."

"Hubert's not really a relative, Jaimie."

"She is."

"What do you mean by that?"

"She's your little sister, mother. How can you block like that?"

Mother reacted with that special surprise that people show when they suddenly find out that everything fits.

"Why didn't they tell me?"

"I suppose they thought you knew. He called her Marge."

"There's something else that I block on . . . why an attractive young woman who apparently has everything would marry Hubert? Can you please tell me? There must be some simple explanation that escapes me."

"As a matter of fact there is. She just told me. Because he's like Gramps."

"Like Gramps! Hubert, of all people? Why?"

"He knows how to love."

Lorie

There were two things in the gallery that always disturbed Lorie, neither of which Jaimie took seriously because he didn't at all understand how close Lorie's feelings were to his own. To begin with, she didn't like her title. Not that she had formally been given a title nor did Jaimie ever use one, but sometimes shoppers would refer to her as his secretary and although this designation of rank was more often than not prefixed with the word *charming*, to her way of thinking it remained a stigma.

The second grievance also had to do with something that was said, although in all probability Lorie never heard it. But then she didn't have to – for it was the opinion of some of Jaimie's intellectual friends that Lorie wasn't intelligent or at any rate they considered her attitude frivolous, especially in regard to painting. Jaimie had never claimed that Lorie was particularly intelligent nor was he disturbed by what his friends called her "nonsense". The trouble was, from Lorie's point of view, he wasn't sufficiently disturbed by the charm that covered it up.

From the first day in the hotel room when, in answer to his advertisement, she had come to be interviewed and he had employed her to help him open his gallery, he had suspected that she was faking, that her interest in modern painting was ready-made, but she had charm and a great flair for the curiously beautiful which showed both in her reaction to what he had shown her and in her elegantly simple dress. And she had wanted the job so badly; in fact it was this desperation that had decided him. In the months that followed, his mind sometimes reviewed the more "cultured" foreign girls, any one of whom might have made him a better shopkeeper, but he never had serious reason to regret his choice.

Even with the years it had been a successful partnership although, naturally enough, they were often annoyed with one another. In retrospect the crux of this annoyance had centered, apparently at least, around a sense of snobbery. They were like two people in the process of changing convictions and the field of snobbery was still their meeting ground. It was on this field that Lorie had first openly faced him when, during the second year, Jaimie had point-blank refused to go to some great collector's house.

"Why not?" Lorie had asked in a tone that clearly wanted no answer.

"Oh I did that the first year," Jaimie had said. "I admit that's probably one reason why I started the place. But now I've met them. If I can't sell pictures without shaking hands, then I won't sell them."

"Well, then you won't sell them," Lorie had said with finality and went into her little office. He lacked the assurance to let it drop and followed her in.

"Why don't you go?"

"I would if I were asked," she had said bitterly. It was true, for in the years that followed, as she was invited, she went. Yet on those evenings it wasn't the gallery she was selling, poor girl, no matter how much she thought so.

Still there was nothing vulgar in her dealing because she was too diffuse. She was even unaware of her certain instinct for money. Nevertheless it was there and it was amazing how many exorbitantly rich men, young and old, waited on her. She gave promise of wearing extravagant clothes as well as she wore her shopped-for numbers and she had the patter of culture and in those days she was really wonderfully gay. But what attracted them essentially was their sense of safety : even though she might take one in the end, they knew she would never force a showdown.

Each year in the gallery (in view of what happened later, Jaimie remembered) Lorie would be upset by the parade of furs on winter days. After a woman had gone out, she would say, "Did you see that coat?" and the envy of it must have made her ill for she would draw back into the cubbyhole of an office. Jaimie didn't take her sorrow seriously although once he said, "Do they really mean that much? Well, someday you can have them if you want." And she had said, "Oh, never" so softly, almost to herself, like a great pain for love that one cannot speak out loud.

48

Jaimie thought afterwards that perhaps this envy was not so strange. After all she had been a poor girl in a rich girls' college, and a prom girl at that, not a girl to while-away the weary hours in study. And she had had this zest for pleasure, little pleasures, dresses, dancing, music and bouquets. She knew nothing like the rest who prick the myth but at least she had come away with more than most: she still wanted to learn, a little anyway. But she didn't know how, and so, in fright, she married. And then, after the presents had worn away, it was the same thing. She was poor again and pretending and wanting. That was why she was so desperate about working in the gallery; it was a way out, not permanently, but an island, a resting place between two streams. Perhaps that was all she wanted, a pleasant pretty resting place.

The summer Lorie went to Paris – it was all of a piece and yet her coat too had many colours – she didn't take up with Jaimie's friends who were poets and painters but with his social friends. This group was well-born and charming, even gifted in enthusiasm. Its members had meant a great deal to Jaimie once, their acceptance of him had had a particular meaning because he was then fresh from the affront of Harvard and he was a Jew, but having tasted the dish he had sensed that in spite of the delicacy it was not what he would always be needing. But Lorie, who for want of wealth had known a similar exclusion, not only rose to the bait but swallowed it.

There was still the relief though of the island to come back to. It was an alive little island, in those days called an *avante-garde* gallery, but it was better than that: it drew the doers as well as the voyeurs and so it kept its head up. In consequence, considering the time, there was a great deal of talk about psychoanalysis and again some of it was first-hand. But even the idea of mental therapy was distasteful to Lorie and she would say, "What's the use of it?" meaning "*I* don't need it." It might have appeared that she didn't. But the curious thing is that later, like the social people, she swallowed it whole, again with no proper digestion.

It may be true that people learn only by defeat but this much, at least, is certain: after defeat people must act or perish. Lorie's action then, in applying for a job (which was a great break from her fantasy of social position) had been provoked by the disappointment of her marriage. Similarly, her dismissal from this job led her to act again – but with a difference in timing because in this instance it was not of her choosing. Not that she hadn't been forewarned, for as Jaimie had been running out of money, she had been cautioned that he might have to try to keep the gallery going without her. But when the blow fell, just because she had paid no mind, it seemed cruelly abrupt. In any case, she took it hard. With the years she had come to feel the gallery was her baby too and so, like all half-tending mothers, she felt it was her dramatic right to die with the child. Perhaps it was. But what troubled her besides the hurt and what she mistook for it was the necessity for action. She had acted so well and so long in and from the gallery that she was tired. Jaimie predicted that she would be forced to marry within the year.

She delayed only to see that other jobs were less pleasant, less glamorous and that her position was insecure because it was not altogether of her making. Without the gallery behind her, she too was less glamorous.

She married so suddenly and so brilliantly in terms of the social scene that she doubtless surprised herself no less than the world. Jaimie was abroad at the time and although he heard that he'd been invited to the select wedding, he wondered about it. His doubt seemed confirmed by the first direct word he had from Lorie. It was a note enclosing a cheque in payment of a small loan, or rather a cheque enclosing a note, for the note in its entirety read, "Enfin Lorie". It repaid him of course for more than the little money. For no matter how he could excuse Lorie, understanding how suddenly great wealth might be embarrassing with old friends and sensing, in this too bitter way, how Lorie was even foreign to herself, what Jaimie would not permit was the understanding of his own hurt.

Sometime later, Lorie and the nickel-plated prince took Jaimie to dinner. Jaimie found him smooth, civil, charming and cold. It was a little awkward except for Lorie, who was preoccupied with showing each man off to the other. Although both men played their parts well, Jaimie could not resist opportunity's knocking and remarked that no one in this world is entitled to more than five millions. It was an absurd amount of course but his fancy, for love of Lorie, had become cordial. The prince, for his part, took it well, although to Jaimie's mild surprise, he did not forthwith leave the restaurant to part with his fortune. Neither did he, however, drop the subject and explained that although a man (he meant his grandfather) might through his own efforts succeed in an enterprise, when it has grown into an empire it becomes so monstrous as to be beyond control. With this admission of irresponsibility the prince showed his hand but Jaimie, by failing to apply the admission to Lorie, again refused to know.

Another time, the year the war began, Jaimie ran across Lorie and they went shopping together. She had one of those little black cars which people of wealth command whenever they visit strange cities. Somehow it struck Jaimie that the taxi-hailing had suited her better. She had not been well, indeed she had been very ill when her child was born, and she seemed strangely disintegrated, in part not there at all. She was having some dealing with arcanum that showed in a new and occult interest in symbols, but there was a misunderstanding somewhere for she was neither seer nor theosophist. What depressed Jaimie more than this distraction, which was familiar from the old days when it had been funnelled into a mad and loving little gaiety, was her appearance. Before, with no jewels save the first heavy wedding-band, she had achieved a singular elegance with her store-bought dress. In this connection Jaimie recalled their laughter the time old Miss Louchenheim had come into the gallery. Miss Louchenheim had a ridiculous elegance of her own, a combination of clothes-fussiness and continental snobbery, and on seeing Lorie had gone into a rigmarole about having purchased the same model, but not in the original material, and how she felt that this was always, in the end, a mistake. Lorie had said, "I'm very pleased that you like it" or perhaps even "that *you* like it", for she was polite. Miss Louchenheim had come back with, "Why – aren't you true to your own taste? I'm never pleased when people admire my clothes; I like to think mine is better than theirs."

So that was it too perhaps : Lorie was false in her real jewels. With her great fortune, she had of course the taste not to wear fabulous pearls, but even so the charms with their emerald eyes were somehow all wrong.

After shopping Lorie invited Jaimie to dinner and for the second time he was sure she wanted to impress him. For the second time she succeeded for the guests were a mixture of old Paris friends and literary people whom he was pleased to meet. There was a certain amount of drinking and afterwards, when the evening was ready to wind up in a friend's place, Lorie must have been tight. Suddenly, in front of everyone, she said, "Jaimie thinks I'm unhappy. Yes, isn't it strange, but

Jaimie thinks I'm unhappy." There was some defiance in what she said, some patronage too that in the semi-public showing embarrassed Jaimie, but under it an old affection and through this feeling he could see beyond the others toward the depth of her misery and that she, in her unhappy way, was almost thanking him for seeing.

The following week Jaimie took Lorie to dinner. He had no conviction that their old fondness would be suddenly revived but it was worth tending. And since her unguarding he wanted to help her. Perhaps he would reassure her that he still liked her for herself, in spite of her wealth, and prove it by asking no favour.

Lorie suggested a little bistro for dinner and Jaimie went with misgiving, wondering what she would now consider a "bistro" and more distressed than amused by her half-French way of talking. Did money, he could not help but also wonder, do this too? But the place turned out to be a real bistro miraculously transplanted in the west forties and true to Lorie's old gay taste. It was crowded, not in the stand-in-line-are-important-people-here way, but agreeably . . . even the noise was a personal noise. They began drinking at the bar and by the time they got a table Lorie was already tight. She immediately, in some mysterious way, picked up a French sailor and commanded him, again by a kind of conjuring – for there was no apparent communication – to leave his table and come over for a drink. She told him he had beautiful eyes. Then she took one of the jewelled bands from her finger, gave it to him and dismissed him. "The joke is," she said to Jaimie – it was all in French now – "that he doesn't know they are real."

But although Lorie seemed so miserably disintegrated she was nevertheless quick to the horror in Jaimie's eyes, for she tried to divert the joke by repeating it: "Don't you want one?" she said handing him another ring.

Jamie fondled the ring. With so much to say he was struck dumb. It seemed suddenly as if all the sorrow in the world had come to sit at their little table but it sat between them rather than with them and Jamie could not get through. Until then he had felt the trouble was Lorie's inaccessibility, as if her presence had been removed, first by so much unhappiness and then again by a film of drink, but now he knew these were superficial coverings and he knew too that the deeper trouble was his own ineptitude, which in turn was based on their joint confusion. And in that moment the parts of the confusion began to piece themselves together as once before, when under ether, patterns of linoleum had passed in review insistent on forming designs.

First of all there was the awful part of his own training, the childhood of incessant money-money – oh, coated with culture but clearly in dollars – which against all volition still called to him and told him, as he fondled the ring, that if he were to take a ring from Lorie it must not be this trinket but a pearl of price. And it made him ashamed, childishly ashamed and bitter to the point of laughing, just as he had always wanted to laugh whenever his father, at the mention of Lorie, would exclaim, "It's a regular Cinderella story."

And in going back to his own childhood Jaimie wondered back to hers. Lorie must have always had what is called personality but besides that, what was she like? Probably very loving and somehow always very unsure. Something certainly must have happened very early, for the contortion was there but so deep rooted and covered with the smooth bittersweet leaves of charm that it was hard to know. Jaimie had never seen Lorie's father but, from her way of speaking about him, she must have loved him very much. He had been a country doctor with a reputation and he always sounded as if there were no question of his integrity. He sounded in fact like a first-rate country doctor, a gentleman who perhaps put too much stock in a gentleman's reputation. Perhaps too by the time she was old enough to have what he considered problems he had become exhausted by other people's problems.

Lorie's mother, whom Jamie had once met, gave no direction for an answer except that she suggested mild timidity but then she was deaf and like some deaf people put up a protective screen. Her wavelengths carried a gentleness which was repeated in her younger daughter, Con. Like Lorie, Con had charm but she was both healthier and easier than Lorie and gave the impression that when the time came she would not hold back from pleasure. There seemed no competition between them, not even when Con's beaux were around, about whom Lorie was a little patronising, but both pleasantly and foolishly so, as if it were something she had gone through and therefore inevitable. It was so easy it was misleading.

What then had happened? With Lorie there before him, the answer seemed suddenly ready like a long-forgotten word on the tip of the tongue. For in the instant, in playing with the ring, Jaimie had looked through it to sight the fretting on Lorie's dress, but what he saw was too immediate – his eyes were held but his understanding had to let go, like a memory that has to work back before it becomes clear. So he went back to the loneliness of her childhood, a childhood of love perhaps but with a deficiency in kind, a wearing-down, as if Lorie's parents had given up with her coming. And then the vision in the ring took focus. It was this same dress that had been denied her long ago – oh it made no matter when (one time perhaps when a boy from some big house on the hill had asked her to the cotillion). What mattered that time was that she must have said she was sick and although she thought she was pretending, she was sicker than anyone knew, from an ailment that she could never quite shake off again, although forever afterwards there was the bravery of her gaiety to fool people with.

Jaimie put down the ring and looked at her. "Well," he thought bitterly, "Now she's got the dress."

Lorie looked back. There had been a time when she had been generous with Jaimie and his dreams, for in spite of seemingly to be left out, in her heart she had known she was always somehow part of them. But since then there had been too much disappointment, there was no room now for patience and besides, she had caught a material aspect in the look. Their love had always practised this kind of sensibility but in place of consummation it was doomed, as now, to misfire. For in registering his look, Lorie quite naturally mistook the dress for the ring, thinking that he had taken all this while to decide whether or not to keep it. So what should have been insight came out exasperation as she said, "Well, make up your mind."

Jaimie did. He thought it was too late and hopeless, and anyway there is nothing more infectious than anger. He took her home.

In the cab Lorie's drink, exposed to air, seemed to precipitate her dissolution. She kept repeating something about "the next time someone wants to give you something real" and Jamie couldn't wait to reach her door. In shameful haste he helped her up the stairs and left.

But the evening with Lorie was not quite over. There was something wrong too in the sailor's possession of the ring. So Jaimie went back to retrieve it. But the bistro's mock-gaiety for that night was also over ... there were the parting stragglers, the piled chairs and oxide suds, but the sailor, like the Smyrna merchant, had gone, leaving no address.

Walking through the after-disappointment of the city streets, Jaimie felt the kind of childish relief that comes with the knowledge of having broken something. It is final, a thing done, and yet it is impermanent, for there is the settlement to come. But for what? And by whom? He didn't know. He knew only that the late city was like the forest, for at night the traffic of both has stopped, the bird cries and hawkers' cries are over – at least for this morning's hour – and at last there is nothing to come between. So he looked into the sailor's eyes. They seemed to belong to the boy who long ago had asked her to the cotillion. And then they changed to Rudi's, Rudi of the gallery days, the one among all the suitors who had been worth anything and who, in his too easy way, had almost brought her home. Yes, Lorie had loved Rudi but there had been something wrong with that too. And then, although Jaimie again looked into the eyes, he still didn't see the reflection.

Jaimie never saw Lorie again. But in a sense, he spent one more evening with her. It was at a party, given as it turned out for Rudi and his new wife, and on sight of Jaimie Rudi had ignored everyone almost to embrace him with talk of Lorie. It was strange, for he had spoken in anger and for anyone who might choose to hear. At first it had seemed an indiscretion but as he went on there had been relief for Jaimie too, for Rudi had not only been voicing his own grievance but Jaimie's as well – he'd just been waiting to spill it on someone who had also loved her. But the strangest part of all was that Rudi had spoken as if she were dead.

"I have known several people of great wealth," Rudi had said, "and the same thing undoes them all. They surround themselves with a court and that's the beginning of the end. My God, it's vanity, I suppose, but Lorie should have known better. Look at the people she met in your gallery. Why didn't she come back to them for her projects? She could have done such wonderful things."

"And have had such pleasure doing them," Jaimie had been about to say, for he had always hoped she would have come to him. But just then a voice said, "I've always been sorry for *him*." As if they had been talking quite privately, together they had turned in anger. It was Rudi's wife.

"Oh I never knew Lorie, but from all I hear she must have been very charming." She had said it surprisingly with no edge. "But don't you really know about her father-in-law? How he dragged the mother through all the courts? Of course I know because I came from the same little town. He tried to change the laws by buying the state legislature –

and almost succeeded. But with all his millions he couldn't beat her. Oh he finally got rid of her somehow – the thing went on and on – but what I remember is the guards and locked gates. And think how hideous it must have been for the boy inside.

"I've been told that girls who marry their fathers are fortunate," and she smiled at Rudi. "Somehow it isn't supposed to work the other way around. But isn't that what happened? Hasn't Lorie's husband, now that his father is dead, put on the old man's shoes? His mother also came from another 'class' – and she too probably once was fresh and wonderful. But his father couldn't take it either apparently, and so, in his way, destroyed her. It's this repetition – like a curse, I think – that's the saddest of all about the world."

It was glib – but it was true. The prince had married Lorie to unlock the gates. She was something he had dreamed of, different, gay, not dressed in finishing-school clothes. But for this perception alone Lorie would not give the difference. She let him, perhaps even helped him, make her over against his heart's desire. So she bought fashionable houses and bred afghans, and dogs had always made her physically ill. The prince knew this, so was it any wonder that later, like the jingle, the girl outlived the mad dog's bite, and then she calmly died of fright?

Jaimie read about it in the paper far away. Lorie's old sweetness came through in the news photograph but Jaimie was even more shocked because of a strange circumstance. The evening before he had opened a crate containing the first paintings around which he had made his gallery's collection. They were a curious assembly, so interwoven with his past that he could form no evaluation of their qualities. He had unpacked them all the time thinking of Lorie and how these duds-to-the-trade had turned up regularly at the yearly inventory, sometimes in broken frames and with broken glass, and how, with a mixture of disgust and delight, Lorie would holler at them, making them seem personal and ashamed at being so unwanted. So through the misunderstanding and destruction the pictures had brought her back to him that evening very closely.

And the next day there had been the newspaper notice. He had thought then that perhaps after all there was something in the nonsense of her mystic symbols, those rings and crosses she had hit upon after her analysis, and somehow he believed she would have liked it very much.

It wasn't Lorie's death alone that made Jaimie sad – for to him in the distance she had been so miserable – but the terrible waste of love. He felt he should write someone – who but the nickel-plated prince? – but besides the usual apathy about a condolence note there was the question of whether to be conventional and civilised or warm and real. Finally he wrote and, although he stayed within the bounds of decorum, he chose the warmer way and wrote about the coincidence of the paintings. Somehow he felt, absurdly, that the prince would think he was trying to sell them.

For his pains he received an engraved acknowledgment. But wasn't it also something more? Wasn't it an acknowledgment – oh, yes, with her acquiescence perhaps but an acknowledgment nevertheless, cold and plain – that the prince had killed her?

But what then about Rudi? And what for that matter about himself? For wasn't it he and no other who long ago had taken her by the hand to show her the happy land and left her afraid to lead her in? Oh surely the prince had bargained for more and shown himself shamefully ignorant, and this, for all time, was enough for Jaimie to hang his hatred on. For otherwise there would have been no way out.

The way out, though, wasn't to be that easy. For at the end of the summer, when Jaimie came back to his flat, there on the tray in front of the mirror, among the second-class matter, was the letter in the familiar hand. Its date was blurred and the stamp had come loose, which probably explained why it had not been forwarded. He sat down in the cold stillness and opened it very carefully. Then slowly, in breathlessness, he read,

> I would have liked to see you again but I guess
> it's not important, or not important for me.
> But for you, Jaimie – the next time someone
> wants to give you something real, take it.
> Goodbye my darling. Enfin –
>
> LORIE

He held the letter as if time had stopped, aware only of the trembling in his fingers. But time had not stopped and he had looked up and was staring in the glass. There through the dust he saw the sailor's eyes and knew at last his own.

The Gold Star

That evening when Giovanni called from downstairs Jaimie had no idea who he could be. Even when he had said, "You helped me in Italy after my mother died", it explained nothing, because of all the men who had come into that Red Cross Tent . . . there were hundreds of them . . . most had come because of bad news from home.

Of course when he saw him he immediately knew him and remembered all about him. He was a tall, dark, remarkably handsome man and, at the Replacement Depot, after Jaimie had told him about his mother, he'd sat there, crumpling the telegram, then smoothing it out and crumpling it again. He had obviously wanted to talk but he didn't know how to begin. Finally he'd come out with it. He was thinking of deserting because he couldn't face killing any more. He was of Italian descent, he'd come up through Italy since the first Sicilian landings, it had been like killing his own people, but it wasn't only that, he hated killing anyway, and now, with the war almost over, it made no sense. Anyway, if they sent him up front again, he wanted no part of it.

"Giovanni! How'd you ever know how to find me?"

"I went to the head Red Cross office in Washington. They were a little ornery until I showed them, thanks to you, my honorable discharge."

He looked older and there was a certain sadness about him that somehow was almost touching. He was so tired that white showed around the gills.

"Would you like a drink?"

"Yes, thank you. I came because of how you helped me before. This time I'm in real trouble. Straight, please. I don't know how to tell you. Here," and he took a newspaper clipping from his pocket.

Jaimie looked at it and then at him.

"You don't know how bad I feel. I loved her, I know that now. She made me feel as if I belonged to someone. Why do you look at me like that?"

"My mother came from Jackson. It's a small town . . . she probably knew Elsie. I often heard her name, Elsie Wojevec. What you need, Giovanni, is a lawyer."

"I'm not sure it'd help."

They talked until morning. He had the money Elsie had given him in his pocket. He hadn't touched it. There were no witnesses; there would be no evidence of violence. He was a war veteran; that, plus the fact that if on his own initiative he went to the authorities . . . or better, if his lawyer went . . . would all be in his favor.

"I don't see the problem," Jaimie said, "Except how you feel. I understand that. You feel such remorse. But it was an accident. There'll be no question about it. How can there be? All you need is a good lawyer. My father's a lawyer and he'll know who's best for this."

"Yes, but it will look as if I planned it anyway, won't it? There was no record of me, no photograph. Even the car she gave me was in her name, Wojevec. Who will believe that it was her idea that I didn't use my right name?"

"It doesn't make any difference who believes it; it's so unimportant. I don't have to be a lawyer to know that much. You're magnifying everything because you feel guilty . . . and have such a feeling of loss too. For the same reason you resist having a lawyer. Otherwise it doesn't make sense. But if you don't have a lawyer, what'll you do?"

"Oh, Canada or Australia."

"Isn't that dangerous?"

"Why? If they don't know my name yet, the odds are they'll never know it."

"I'm not so sure about the odds. For one thing, if Elsie, as you say, was so possessed with money, wouldn't she have had a will? And as she loved you, wouldn't she have left everything to you or something anyway? Legally she would have used your real name."

"Yes, I guess she would, but it wouldn't prove anything. Who would know who I am? Sure, the money'd be nice but after what happened I don't know that I want it. I don't know that I want the money in my pocket, and that's a fact." He got up. "I never thought about a will. But if Elsie did leave me her money and she had a lot, wouldn't they say that I knew about it?"

"That's all the more reason to call a lawyer right away."

"Let me sleep on it. I'm too tired to decide anything now anyway. I'll call you in the morning."

When old Mr. Bender told Elsie Wojevec about the legacy she couldn't believe her ears. All that money and her mother had never said a word.

"And you're sure she knew about it?"

"I told her myself. It was not so long after you were born."

"And she knew all the terms?"

"That she had the right to the income during her lifetime? Certainly she knew it."

"Then why, when we could have used it, didn't she touch it?"

"As she knew that the principal was yours, I presume it was because she also knew that with the accrued interest it was sure to grow. Your mother must have loved you very much for such a sacrifice."

Was he joking? Her mother had wanted to chain her to her sickbed, and she had. That's why she never touched the money. Just to think! With the income her mother could have had a practical nurse and Elsie could have had dresses and gone to parties like other girls. Why, she would have been free to marry.

"It's been to your advantage, whatever her reason, as the capital has more than doubled; and now it's all yours, Elsie, with no strings tied. Have you any questions?"

Yes, but as the bequest had been anonymous old Mr. Bender, even if he knew, would never answer them: who was her father? Had Mr. Bender known him? What was he like?

"The capital, in my opinion, has been too conservatively invested. Our advisory service should now reconsider the entire fund and send you its recommendation. You can study it, there's no hurry, and tell us at your leisure."

"I can tell you now. Leave it. It's done very well, and with mother gone, what purpose would it serve? Alone I can support myself very nicely."

"Why should you? Unless you want to go on dressmaking. You'll find money can buy quite a lot. What would you like most?"

"Not what money could buy." Mr. Bender thought she meant love.

Perhaps she did but she wasn't thinking about it. She was thinking about dressmaking and what pleasure it gave her, and, because she was so gifted at it, the pleasure it gave others, but at the same time how she hated the patronage that came with it, the feeling of being indexed as a half-caste as the lunch served upstairs on a tray always evidenced. Oh no, it was never suggested that she eat with the servants, but she was seldom invited in the dining room and, if she was, it was worse because she was there on sufferance. What she wanted was what her mother sewing in the big houses before her had wanted: respect.

'Why don't you give yourself a vacation anyway, Elsie? You can certainly afford it. You've never been abroad. Or why not take a cruise?"

"I'll think about it."

After thirty years of washing her own hair it was heaven having Mabel fuss over her and remark on what gorgeous long hair she had and fix her so comfy under the drier and bring her the latest mags. Mabel thought that because Elsie was a dressmaker she'd want *Vogue* and *Harper's Bazaar* and Elsie never corrected her but she was forever looking at fashions in the homes of her ladies and so she'd turn to the ads and travel photos at the back. With her mother ill so long she had never gone anywhere.

COME TO GARDENIA, THE GARDEN CITY! !

How beautiful it looked with pink rhododendrons and California poppies and sagebrush and Hawaiian lehua and sego lilies. The names were under the flowers and the colors were the same in the humming birds and butterflies, all bright and gay against the little white houses.

COME TO GARDENIA, EDEN ON EARTH, AND BE HAPPY! ! !

"Doesn't it look wonderful out of this cold?" Mabel yelled and then switched off the drier. "If I didn't have the family, I'd take off and go, believe me. But you." She ran the comb through Elsie's hair. "With your mother gone, why don't you go? I would."

"It's not half dry, Mabel."

"I know. I'll bet you're the only one in that fancy sewing circle with long hair. Why don't you let Mr. Hale cut it? It'd take ten years off your looks. It's your turn, Elsie, everybody knows how you lived for your mother. And Mr. Hale's the best there is; he doesn't have to work anymore he made so much in Hollywood . . . you know, fixing up the stars."

Elsie smiled. "I'm not a star."

"Listen, Elsie, he's not a stylist, he's an artiste. No woman who ever had her hair bobbed by Jerry Hale ever regretted it. I give you my hand on it."

"I don't know."

"I do," Mabel said and called, "Oh Jerry."

"What gorgeous raven locks," Mr. Hale said, taking a strand. He laughed. "It would be a crime to cut them, now wouldn't it?" and then snip, half of them were off.

Elsie's heart turned over. She couldn't believe it like when Mr. Bender told her about the money.

"You're going to be a stunner," Mr. Hale said. "Here, give me that costume jewelry," and he chose two pearl earrings. "With your sallow complexion you're right to wear black. . ."

"She's in mourning," Mabel said.

"Oh, I'm sorry . . . see how the white sets off the color and pulls the ears down the way I want. We need a light permanent, Mabel, only here . . ."

"But . . ."

"Yes, I know," Mr. Hale said, "It was beautiful straight but you're different now. You're going to be my masterpiece. I'm terribly excited."

"I do look younger."

"Just you wait, honey," Mabel said. "You'll be a knockout. I'd like to be a mouse in your exclusive sewing bee when you come in. How did you get in with that bunch anyway?"

"I'm a good sewer."

"Oh come on."

"People are more democratic since the war, don't you think?"

"Not with me."

"I don't know; it just happened. I was registering the night after Pearl Harbor with Mrs. Reynolds and the rest of them and Mrs. Reynolds afterwards asked me to come over and sew. So I went. They're very nice to me."

"They should be. You give your professional time. You knew most of them anyway from your dressmaking . . ."

"Some of them. And yet I feel out of it."

"Then they're not so nice to you."

"They talk about their menfolk all the time. They all have somebody in uniform. Even poor Ella Eggers had . . ."

"Isn't it terrible?"

"I'm sick about it."

"You knew Larry . . ."

"I went to school with him. I just loved Larry. Everybody did. And Ella! He was everything to her."

"She was sister and mother and . . ."

"What'll she do?" and Elsie began to cry. "I don't know whether to go over and call or not."

"She won't be sewing with you tonight, poor thing. Don't look at yourself until I rinse it again. Then all the stiffness'll come out."

Back under the drier Mabel handed Elsie the same magazines but she didn't look at them. She was thinking of Larry and Ella because she was heartsick for Ella even though she had become so jealous of her at the Thursday Night Circle that she had begun to hate her. It was because of that feeling of being excluded and wanting respect. For back at the start of what Mabel called "that fancy sewing bee", Elsie had felt that finally, even if by chance, she had been accepted by the women who had always patronized her. And in that first flush of patriotism after Pearl Harbor, it was true, she had been accepted, but then gradually there were innuendoes, little differences, actual distinctions and, as if to ward them off, in her mind at least she had allied herself with Ella because like her Ella was unmarried and also worked for a living. But the likeness was skin-deep, for Ella was respected for all kinds of reasons beginning with birth and culminating with Larry, because with Larry Ella like the others had a man in service, and Elsie was alone again as if lunch as always was being served upstairs.

Mabel finished combing and brought the earrings and put them on and called, "Oh Mr. Hale."

"You're class, honey," Mr. Hale said, "Real class. Let's try this," and he took a flesh-colored lipstick. "I've done what God didn't" and, as if from on high, he admired his creation. "Somebody else'll have to give you the mink coat, that's all . . . it'll top it off." He patted her cheek. "I guess they'll be fighting to give it to you now."

Elsie gasped. She couldn't believe it: she looked so wonderful. Maybe life hadn't gone by after all.

Mr. Hale's beautifying made Elsie late for the Thursday Night Circle. The ladies were already seated and listening to the seven-thirty broadcast. They were so intent they hardly saw her come in. It was about the Italian landings and Elsie wondered if poor Ella would be listening at home. Maybe Larry had been killed in a place like that. The women all had someone, if not there, some place. What if Elsie had someone? Maybe a brother like Larry. Or a son. She was old enough to have had a son. What would he be like? She couldn't imagine but she guessed how intent she'd be listening to the broadcast. She was intent! She was so intent on what the announcer had been saying that she didn't register when he'd finished and Mrs. Reynolds got up to switch off the radio. But Mrs. Reynolds had registered her new look. "Why, Elsie! Look, girls, at Elsie."

Everyone ohed and ahed and Mrs. Beauchamp started to say, "Why Elsie, you're perfectly stun . . ." and then they all hushed and went back to their sewing. Ella had come in.

The women always chatted as they sewed but you could have heard a pin drop. Ella was as white as a sheet. Elsie wanted to reach out and touch her or put her arms around her or say something. She could have hung her head in shame too, because in spite of everything she was still jealous of the respect Ella had, for having gone to college, for being head librarian, for having brought up Larry so well, and now, although it was an awful thing to be jealous of, she'd have more respect for having lost him. She'd have a gold star. Elsie could never have respect like that. Or could she? She could if she had a son. She could never say she had a son in Jackson but . . . in Gardenia, where nobody knew her, with all those flowers . . .

Mrs. Reynolds broke the dream. "Would you like some coffee, Ella?"

"No, thank you."

After that they talked or tried to. There were awkward pauses. Once Cora Collins said, "I expect you next week, Elsie. Caroline will be back and needing everything as usual."

"I'm afraid I can't come."

"Why?"

"I have family obligations. I have to leave Jackson." The words came to her without thinking.

"I hope not for good, Elsie," Mrs. Reynolds said.

"I don't know yet."

Ella left before Mrs. Reynolds served the refreshments and Elsie couldn't bear to see her go like that, for she knew more than the others what it meant to be alone, and so she jumped up and went after her.

"But this isn't your direction, Elsie."

"I know," Elsie said and went on with her anyway. They didn't speak until they came to Ella's door.

"Would you like me to come up with you, Ella?"

"Do."

The flat had books everywhere. It was crowded with furniture that Elsie thought she remembered from the Eggers' old house near the school. An album with loose photographs around it was on the table; it was open at a picture of Larry in a sailor suit. He must have been about twelve then. In the white suit with the swimming eyes and half come-on smile he was an incredibly beautiful boy. Elsie couldn't take her eyes away. If she ever had a son and could choose, he would look like that. She smiled, so lost in imagined affection that Ella surprised her. "Would you like to have it?"

"Oh, but . . ."

"Take it. I have duplicates, another album full. Take another, Elsie, do. You were always so fond of him."

As second choice Elsie took a small round picture of baby Larry in curls.

"My father carried one like that in his watch. But oh, I didn't notice . . . I don't notice anything. I didn't see you had your coat on. Take it off."

"It's all right, Ella."

"With your hair cut, you look so young . . . and pretty. It's no wonder Larry used to talk about you so much."

"That was long ago."

"Tell me what you remember about him."

"Oh so many things. Most of all how he used to sing the same song over and over . . . *I've Got the Whole World in My Hand*. I think he had the Marion Anderson record . . ."

"It's still here."

"Could we play it?"

She knew just where it was. She put it on and Marion Anderson sang about everybody's sorrow, hers and Ella's and Elsie's too someday when maybe she would have to lose her son. It made Elsie want to cry, for Larry, for everything, for Ella sitting there all held in. The song was trying to comfort her and Elsie wanted to help her so much that she began to cry. She felt Ella watching her and looked up and took her hand. And then Ella let go. She cried and cried and Elsie cried with her until the song ended and the needle began to scratch on the same place.

Ella couldn't stop crying and so Elsie said, "I'll bet you haven't eaten all day, Ella. Come on into town with me; we'll find some place open."

"Oh no. I just couldn't. But you should go if you're leaving tomorrow."

"Are you all right?"

"When you and Larry were at school, you were such good friends. I never really knew you . . . nor at the library either all the years you came in to get books . . . but now I feel close to you too. No one could have helped me more. I thought I would never feel anything again, but I do. I hope you'll come back, Elsie, but wherever you are you'll always be in my heart."

Although it was almost eleven when Elsie got home, she telephoned Mr. Bender. No, she hadn't disturbed him. He was all sympathy. No, there would be no problem about travellers checks in the morning, but why bother? He could send Eddie Reece over with what currency she needed, she had her checkbook anyway, and, in case of emergency, she could always contact the bank. It was no trouble, on the contrary an important client was entitled to red carpet treatment, ha ha. And in regard to renting her flat, Eddie happened to be the best possible person. But why, might he ask, was she of all people going by bus? Well, yes, he supposed it was a good way to see the country, but fatiguing. Bon voyage.

She put Larry's pictures on the bed-table and opened the drawer with her mother's rings. She would wear the wedding ring. As to the other ring, of uncut stones that her father had brought back from Italy, or so the story went, she had always assumed it was fake. But in view of all the money she looked again. The uncut stones had the subdued glitter of gentility like her own new look that probably also stemmed from her father, whoever he had been. She admired herself in the mirror, with one ring, with both of them, without any. She wanted to get out of Jackson, away from everything that reminded her of it, but she would wear both rings. "Well, Elsie dear," she said to herself in the glass, "It's all settled : you're lovely and rich and free, and you'll have a boy and he'll be more than poor Ella had, he'll be your own son and you'll be respected for him and not, please God, ever on sufferance again." She got in bed, took up Larry's baby picture, kissed it, whispered, "Good night, my darling" and turned out the light.

Elsie had forgotten how young and agreeable and good-looking Eddie Reece was. He said that with the Hayes plant working night shifts there'd be no trouble renting the flat, and as to getting rid of everything she didn't want, nothing could be easier, all he had to do was telephone the Salvation Army. He eyed the sewing machine and called it "a museum piece" and when she asked him if he'd like it, he said "Would I !" and kissed her. He said she looked wonderful with her hair bobbed, too elegant to go by bus and with so little luggage. He insisted on taking her to the depot.

Elsie first told her story to the woman next to her. Since the bus pulled out of Jackson, the woman had pumped her, and so finally Elsie let her have it.

"Oh, all my life I heard that Gardenia was beautiful and so I decided to live there. You see my husband died when my boy was a baby," and Elsie gave the same brave smile that her mother used to give for the same story. "And I brought up my son sewing . . . I'm a dressmaker and I can find work anywhere, I hope . . . and now he's overseas and it's been so cold and lonely in the house. We were always together . . . you know, his not having a father . . . I just couldn't stand it anymore. So I'm going to start all over. I just have to; it got so I thought I would never feel anything again."

The woman was wide-eyed in admiration. "What's your boy's name?"

"Oh, I call him son. But his real name is Larry."

"Have you a picture of him?"

"Albums full." Elsie took out the round photograph of Larry with curls. "His father used to carry it around in his watch."

"What a pretty boy! Is he still so good-looking?"

"He's handsome."

"He's blond and you're dark but you can see he's yours all right."

"So they say."

After that it was easy. She never repeated verbatim; she was too good a storyteller. She improvised and perfected. Everyone believed her. She half-believed herself. By the time she arrived in San Francisco the Jackson dressmaker had become the owner of a fashionable shop. She had to dress accordingly. She bought only in the best stores with an eye for copying and she made arrangements for materials later on. As she was given a professional discount the rebate on a mink coat made it irresistible. When she stepped off the train in Gardenia she was an elegant woman and happy about it for Larry's sake as well, because, as the man had said the night before, "He must be real proud of a mother like you."

Gardenia wasn't anything, not from the station anyway, just old houses and a run-down hotel. She had been foolish to come so late, it was getting dark. She locked her bags in a station locker and walked up the road to where there was greenery and soon there were little white houses with flowers too. The evening air was cold but instead of bracing her it revived the fatigue from the sudden leaving and the long trip and the buying in San Francisco; Elsie was so tired she wondered if she could make it back to the hotel. Then she saw the tourist sign. It was in the window of a newly painted, large house with roses in front and along the side. She rang and when a woman answered Elsie said she would take the room sight unseen. The woman asked about luggage and Elsie said she'd left it at the station.

"You look all in," the woman said.

"I am."

They climbed the stairs to a large front room with a bay window. The room was filled with antique furniture but like the woman it was neat and there was something friendly about it.

"Lie down, dear, and I'll make you some tea."

"I wouldn't want to bother."

"My, it's no bother. Here, let me hang up your beautiful coat. I like a cup of tea myself but I don't like it alone and Mr. Dalkin's away."

Elsie lay back. She had never thought about all the trouble of having a son and wondered if it was worth it.

Coming up with the tea Mrs. Dalkin caught her taffeta skirt on the latch. "Oh dear." She was real upset about it.

"Don't worry. I'll mend it so it won't show. I'm a dressmaker."

"Well, dear, have your tea first."

Mrs. Dalkin must have guessed that Elsie was hungry; there were sandwiches and chowchow and cake and cookies with the tea. "I've eaten," she said. She told Elsie that her husband represented an undertaking concern and traveled a lot. They didn't have any children, it was the cross she had to bear and it got lonesome. That was really why she took in tourists. She used to be in the antique business, it was handy with her husband's getting hold of deceased people's things but she'd mostly given it up.

Elsie finished the tea and inspected the tear. "If only I had one of my electric sewing machines. But don't worry, I can do it anyway, Mrs. Dalkin.

"Delia, call me Delia."

To hide the tear Elsie made a pocket from the material in the hem. While she sewed she told her story and for Delia's benefit she ended with, "And so, on intuition you might say, I hit on Gardenia. It was just too hard on me at home waiting for him all the time. With all the memories of what we used to do together . . . I just couldn't bear it any longer. I've made up my mind not even to mention our home town again. It's very hard for me to talk about it."

"My dear," Delia said. There were tears in her eyes. "I think you'll like it here . . . I have intuition too . . . and be happy, or as happy as you can be without your boy. Whatever's in my power, I'll do. I promise."

Elsie smiled her gratefulness. "I'll put a ruffle around the pocket in the morning. It'll be as good as new."

"It's as good as new now," Delia said. "My, you surely have clever hands" and she kissed Elsie good night.

"When you see her you can judge for yourself, George." Delia poured the coffee. "You stay away all week and then come back and criticize me."

"You don't know anything about her."

"I've been with her since you left. And anyway you can tell the kind of people they are from her boy's picture. Birth will out. She's the perfect mother and a perfect lady. Otherwise do you think I'd have her in the house with you?"

"How can you tell what kind of dressmaker she is from one bloody pocket?"

"I can."

"And so you're going to give her the whole top floor?"

"What good does it do us empty? And what good is that furniture sitting out in the garage? She'll have a beautiful showroom."

"And how's she going to get customers?"

"By dressing me to begin with. It's all arranged, in place of rent for a start."

"Jesus Christ, Delia."

"Listen, she's her own best advertisement. She's a stunning woman and a lovely, extraordinary person."

As it turned out the only catch in Delia's plan was when George did meet her. Perhaps Delia thought that in his own house he wouldn't be such a louse. Elsie, for her part, should have known better; she knew George was a ladies' man and she knew that he liked her – she wasn't that naive – but with all the comings and goings that furnishing her rooms involved, and then on top of it, just after she'd made Delia's ensemble, the excitement of being commissioned to do the Upjohn wedding with the rush of buying an extra machine and hiring extra girls and the trips to San Francisco for models and then again for materials, and the wedding itself, and all the publicity in the local papers about "Gardenia's ingenious couturier" and the orders that came in after it, she didn't have time to catch her breath and then on the stairs there was breath-catching in quite a different way. George had been coming up before that, usually after dinner when Delia was in the kitchen, but there had always been the excuse of fixing something in the fitting room, like rehanging the drapes, or adjusting the cheval glass, or tacking Larry's service flag in the window, or fitting the sliding doors where the models were hung, always something, and besides Elsie had been busy herself and often one of the girls stayed overtime so they weren't even alone.

And then he'd followed her up on the landing and whispered, "Honey, I've wanted you for so long" and grabbed her and pressed her to him. It was terribly exciting like a scene in the movies, but it was disgusting too with his breathing down her neck. And what he said when she got away was even worse. "Why do you play so hard to get? You want me like I want you. I know the symptoms."

"Don't" she said but he came toward her again and didn't believe her until she said, "Go away, George, and don't come up here again."

After that Delia was more attentive than ever and Elsie was sure she had overhead them, because although Delia never mentioned it directly one day she said, "I'd never thought I'd have a friend like you." Certainly she didn't stop singing Elsie's praises and sometimes Elsie would hear her. "Oh no, not Wednesday evening, I'm sure; she's at the *Wives and Mothers of Servicemen* and would never miss a meeting. No, not Tuesday either; she goes regularly to the library – she reads every word about the 5th Army, where it is and I don't know what all. Yes, she's a model of devotion." Or that day when after the fitting Mrs. Upjohn had admired Larry's photograph and Delia had come in and they'd both thought Elsie had left the room. "My dear, it's dedication. Why, do you know his letters don't even come to the house. She has a post office box because she feels it's more intimate and personal. And it's not for herself that she works so hard. It's for her boy when he comes home . . . it's for what she calls his nest egg."

But it was really Delia's dedication that was responsible for the award. Sitting in the crowded room Elsie wondered what her mother would have thought, what Ella and Mrs. Reynolds and the whole Thursday Night Circle would have thought, seeing her in the black faille suit with the linen waist to match Mr. Hale's earrings and the mink over her shoulders, and listening to the mayor as he went on reading from the notes Delia had given him about "Elsie Wojevec's belief in the harmony of the female form expressed in the folds of a gown", about "her father's family, artists who for centuries in Prague served beauty and now Mrs. Wojevec has brought this old-world tradition to Gardenia" (APPLAUSE), and about her ambition "someday to do for the figure of the young mother with child what the Renaissance painters had done, not to conceal it but to clothe it in all its proud beauty". From here on in the mayor was home to the theme of the award, but as he warmed to it Elsie began to cry. For wouldn't the honor and esteem and everything else have to end when the war was over? For without Larry how could she go on? And why had she gone on and on lying? Elsie would rather die than have Delia find out. When the mayor finally wound up his eulogy and Elsie walked to the platform to receive the GARDENIA MOTHER OF THE YEAR AWARD, she managed to control her tears, but everyone else was so moved that you could hear the sniffles until they were drowned out by the burst of applause.

At night, kissing Larry's picture, she cried her heart out. "Oh, my darling, what did they do to you?" and then, sobbing, she came to the real heartbreak. "What will I do without you?" What could she do? Would a death message come from the Army or through the Red Cross and would it be marked with a gold star? She could buy a flag with a gold star or for that matter make one but it was the death message that was essential to be believed and she didn't dare risk saying it had been put in her P.O. box, for in a little town with the star on it word would have got around.

Delia of course knew that Elsie was sick with worry and although Delia never admitted that Larry might be a casualty she sounded the alarm: everyone knew that Elsie had had no letter in months. But preparation was one thing; how to make the message genuine was another. Had she lied herself out? She had the money to start again somewhere else but for what? Away from Gardenia without Larry she could never again have the esteem. Oh, if she were only dead too.

She broke Delia's heart. Each morning she looked so terrible until finally Delia could bear it no longer. "Elsie, what you fear hasn't happened, dear, because if it had you would have had word."

"How?"

"George says you would have been notified through the Red Cross ... automatically."

"But how? Exactly how?"

"No matter how, it hasn't happened, dear. There are so many other possibilities."

"What?"

"Well, he could have been taken prisoner."

"Oh, God."

"Or he could have been wounded."

"Oh no!" Elsie began to moan, but Delia was determined once and for all to speak out.

"Perhaps he was unconscious for a while."

"Don't," Elsie said and her moaning became almost uncontrollable. "Don't go on."

"It's you who can't go on like this. You have to do something, dear."

"I know. My bag's been packed for days. I keep putting it off. I'll go now."

"Where, dear?"

"Sacramento. I'm told there's a man there who's the head of all inquiries for California. I may have a surprise for you when I come back, Delia. Anything is possible, isn't it? Or what would you do, Delia, if I didn't come back at all?"

She spoke so wildly that Delia wanted to go with her but Elsie wouldn't hear of it. "Instead, would you please cancel my fittings? For two days and then we'll see" and she handed Delia her appointment book. "What will you say, Delia?"

"The truth."

"Yes, it's always best."

When Elsie arrived at her hotel in San Francisco she was told Germany had unconditionally surrendered. The announcement completed her disintegration. She had planned to go on to Sacramento with the vague hope that at State Headquarters she might chance on an answer, but she didn't leave her room. She couldn't even think. If she could only bribe a newspaper to print an obituary! Or should she write to Jackson for the original clipping about Larry but with the Eggers name this was crazy. Was she losing her mind? Or being punished because she'd gone too far and lied so much? After two days without any decision she finally made one. She would return to Gardenia for a month or two and then end it. By killing herself? If there was no way out. She didn't want to die but she didn't want to go back without hope either. She let the 4:40 pull out and the 7:30 as well and went back to the hotel. Her room was still free, it was not even made up, the clerk would send the maid.

The maid arrived breathless probably from age although she carried on as if the end of the world had come because the room was still unmade.

"There are worse things," Elsie said and meant it, and explained that it was she who had left the room and come back because she wasn't well.

"Are you in pain, madame?"

"Only here," Elsie said with her hand to her heart, and as the woman straightened the room Elsie told all about Larry.

"You're not a war mother yet," the woman said, "So you've no cause to feel so bad. But my poor sister is. Her one consolation is that later on they say the government is going to send war mothers to Europe to visit the boys' graves, poor things."

The information cheered Elsie up no end. Why hadn't she thought of it?! She didn't need a death message, for she too would go to Europe later and search and finally find Larry's grave. Though poppies grow in Flanders fields. Or even better, why couldn't Larry in the end be the unknown soldier? Perhaps that was going too far, but her imagination was back and with it her appetite. She hadn't really eaten since leaving Gardenia and she had a wonderful dinner and the next day, instead of rushing back empty-handed, she shopped, buying marvellous things including a French original, a black linen suit that fitted her so perfectly she wore it out. At the station she had missed the 4:40, but no matter, as she had missed lunch as well she'd eat something in the station restaurant.

There was no porter and a serviceman asked if he could help her. He took her bag and then her coat and deposited them with her at a table. She thanked him. He was tall but she hardly noticed him.

She ordered and when she looked up she saw the serviceman. He had put a coin in the coffee machine and was bending over to take the cup. He could have been Larry. Her heart turned over. She stared and he saw her. Then she looked away.

He was standing by her table with his cup. "May I sit down?" She didn't look up. "Yes." Her heart was pounding so. She was faint, from hunger probably. Still she didn't look at him. She looked at his hands. They were broad and strong and studded with black hairs and could have been a workman's hands except the nails were clean. She kept

74

staring at them and he knew it. Finally he caught her eye and smiled.

The waitress brought her order and she began eating but it was embarrassing because he watched the food the way he'd watched her.

"Couldn't I order you something . . . the same thing? It's no fun eating alone."

"Thank you."

"The same again," Elsie said to the waitress, and when the girl had gone, "Here, take half and I'll take yours when it comes."

"It's nice of you."

He seemed famished too but controlled and well-mannered. He cut the sandwich into smaller slices and chewed thoroughly with his mouth closed. He was dark and Larry was blond and yet . . .

"Why are you so kind?"

"You're a serviceman like Larry, my son. When I saw you over there my heart stood still . . . you're so like him in many ways." She put her hand over his. "I could only think of him."

"I thought of you differently," the man said. "Yep, differently."

"Are you in service long?"

"I was . . . too long. I'm not good for anything anymore." He laughed but he wanted her in on the joke, whatever it was, because he looked at her as if they were intimate. "Or not for much." He had beautiful teeth.

The girl put down the order. She arranged his plate and cutlery. She didn't want to leave. "Would you all like something to drink?"

"That's an idea. Well, would we?"

"Oh no," Elsie said. "Anyway I invited you."

"So? . . . it's my turn. Vino . . . red wine. Two glasses. Un repas sans vin est un repas perdu."

Elsie didn't understand.

"A meal without wine is a meal lost. That was a sign in a restaurant where I used to eat. Here, in Frisco, near a little theatre. But you don't want to hear about me. Where is Larry now?"

"I don't know that he's anywhere. He may not be alive."

"Oh. I'm sorry."

"I just don't know. I can't find out anything."

"How come? Maybe he's AWOL."

Again Elsie didn't understand.

"Absent without leave."

"Oh no."

"Or POW. Prisoner of War."

"I don't think so." She looked at him so strangely. He liked it. He liked strange women.

The girl brought the wine. "Liquor has to be paid for now."

He took some dollar bills from his pocket and gave one to the girl. "Drink some. It'll do you good," and then looking Elsie in the eyes, "To us. I feel better. I hadn't eaten all day. I'd saved just enough to go to L.A." He reached over and took the food bill. "But now I can't so I might as well pay for this too."

"Oh no. That would make me feel terrible."

"Why? I didn't want to go anyway."

"What are you going to do then?"

"Stay with you."

Elsie was astounded. She'd wanted to be with him since she saw him at the coffee machine. She wanted to be with him even more now because she liked the way he said everything as if it were a factual statement and, besides being so manly and clean, he had such good manners. But she looked at her watch.

"God in heaven. I'll miss my train again."

"Why 'again'?"

"Because I missed three."

He laughed. "Then miss another."

"Oh no." She opened her purse but he reached for the bill and paid it.

"What time does it leave?" and when she told him he said, "You've time to burn" but he picked up her bag with his and again laughed. "You see it looks as if we're traveling together. We're meant to be together, that's all. Why don't you stay here tonight anyway?"

"Oh no," but she was sorry she'd said it so fast.

"Why do you say 'Oh no' to everything?" He put his face down to hers. "Can't you say 'Oh yes'?"

"I should have gone back yesterday. I have appointments . . . fittings. I'm a dressmaker."

"So that's why you look so grand. I just didn't pick up your bag, you know. I was watching you. I like class and that's what you are all right. But if you gotta go, you gotta go," and he started out again. "Have you a husband?"

"Not any more."

"Who's waiting for you at home then?"

They had reached the coach door. He took her hand and patted it. Elsie thought they must look for all the world like lovers. It gave her a thrill. "All right, have it your way, I won't insist. I like you. If you can't stay, can I come with you?"

She was going to say "Oh no" again but caught herself. Why shouldn't he come . . . except for Delia and George. "What would I tell the people downstairs?"

"Do you have to tell them anything?"

"Yes. I haven't been there, in the town, so very long and they'd think . . ."

"The truth. Do they know Larry?"

"No."

"All aboard."

"Then there's no reason," and he got in the car after her as the conductor closed the door.

"Why," she said as the train pulled out, "I don't even know your name."

"Larry."

"I could never tell such a lie." But he thought she could, she seemed so happy.

He was happy too. "I'm crazy about you and you know it. The guys who wrote about love at first sight knew what they were saying, don't you think? I do." He kept patting her hand. "My mom died while I was overseas. You remind me of her a little when I was a kid. Do you think I'm looking for another mother?" He kissed her hand. "It could be, but I don't think so."

It was strange, uncanny even, like opposite pieces that fit in a jigsaw puzzle because he reminded her more and more of Larry.

"What are you afraid of? That your boy might show up?"

"He wouldn't."

"How do you know if you don't know what happened?"

"He couldn't. I'm positive."

He looked at her. Well, he'd figure that one out later. "Then relax. Let me direct this one. I've worked for a lot of lousy directors, not just acting, a grip – that's a stagehand, lighting, everything. All I've got to know is my sides. I won't go up." Again he had to explain.

"Just tell me what to say."

"Italy. You were in Italy."

"Actually I was. Where was I born?"

"They don't know that. They just know that I love you."

He kissed her. "What's your name?"

"Elsie."

"Elsie what?"

"Elsie Wojevec."

"Jesus, how do you spell that?"

Elsie had always been her best advertisement – a handsome, well-dressed woman – but after her boy came back she was really and truly lovely. To see her with her son made people smile just from the happiness of it, for the boy although he was actually a man, seemed as devoted as she. They were a good-looking pair all right – he was handsome with the same dark hair and eyes – and although she was young to have such a mature son, on the other hand the war aged boys so terribly.

The ordeal was in the afternoon. They couldn't wait to touch each other until the door closed after the last fitting. To Elsie, because she had waited all her life for Larry, the minutes lasted forever, and although Larry had had to have discipline in the army, he had never had a woman waiting like this one.

"Give it to me, mom. Christ, you're wonderful, mom. I love you mom."

"My darling."

Delia was at her wits end. "You sound jealous," she said. George could try the patience of a saint when he set his mind to it.

"All I said was, 'There's something rotten in Denmark'."

"What, I'd like to know?"

"The way he hangs around his mother, for one thing. And, if you ask me, she's too crazy about him."

"On account of the war she hasn't seen him for three years, so of course she's crazy about him. And I am too, about both of them."

"Listen, Delia, the sounds I heard coming from upstairs last night didn't sound exactly like a mother and son to me."

78

Delia was furious. "Do you want to know the truth? You're getting to be a dirty old man."

Elsie and Larry spent most of the weekends in San Francisco and Elsie bought her boy a present every time: a sports outfit, a gold watch, an English trenchcoat, a Dunhill lighter and, at Larry's suggestion – "so you won't be ashamed to be seen with me, mom" – tailor-made grey flannels. It was fun to dress him because he was so good-looking. He had a taste for style, but he was practical rather than greedy, and when he also suggested a car, he assumed it would be an old one. He combed the car lots with the same eye for style and utility and when he found one that was a bargain and had class too and rushed back to tell Elsie and get the needful he was livid when she hesitated. He thought it was on account of the price and he was about to let her have it when she said, "Darling, I don't buy old sewing machines or secondhand clothes, for you or me. Why do we buy a secondhand car? I'd like to give you a new one." There were tears in his eyes, he was so ashamed. No one had ever loved him like that.

He chose an Oldsmobile Convertible. BEAUTIFUL. Three thousand bucks.

Back in the hotel he thought it over. "How many dresses will you have to make to pay for it, mom?"

"Darling! Quite a few but . . ."

"Why don't we get the other one?"

She kissed him. "I have a little money put away, enough for this, darling." She opened her checkbook. "Do you know I don't know your name!"

"Giovanni, with two ns. But after now I'm Larry forever more. Wait a minute, mom."

"What, darling?"

"Gardenia's a one-horse town. It might not be so good if anyone sees the registration. Better put it in your name, mom."

She caressed him. How he loved her! She could have cried.

The new car made him restless. He took to driving around, away from Gardenia, up to Frisco mostly and hanging around the theatre, not thinking of anything specially but just to see if there was anyone he knew and sure enough there was Tommy Mercer. Tommy was in on a new theatre group, very talented people, tie-up with Hollywood probably, big deal, technician-backers at a premium.

"You look sharp," Tommy said. "You wanted to be more than a grip. Maybe here's your chance."

"What price la gloire?"

"Ten grand."

"Where would I get that kind of money?"

"Whose car?"

"Mine."

"Well . . ."

It set him thinking.

He knew from the start that Elsie was a liar. Not that he minded; he kind of liked it. It interested him. But was she so crazy as to think he didn't know? It was funny about that picture too when she put it away and he asked, "Why?" "Why on earth, darling, do I need it when I have you?" Well, he supposed she didn't. But was she so screwy as to think he was the same person? She hadn't in the station. Maybe she was a schizophreniac or something. If she was, she was a sweet one . . . and in bed, Christ, he still got hot just thinking about her. And why, if she'd saved it for him all the years and it made her so good, why not keep his big mouth shut if she wanted it that way? He liked to please her because he loved her, it was as simple as that.

If she'd saved up sex and lied about it, what about money? At the station, in that suit and with that coat she'd looked like a million, no doubt about it, but he'd come for the ride or the lark or the lay, because he liked her, for Christ's sake, he was no pimp or gigolo. Or was he? Was that what Mercer meant when he said, "Well . . .?"

On Wednesday, about two weeks after Elsie bought the car, she ran short of material for a rush job and so he drove her down to Frisco. That night Tommy and his wife took them out. They both thought Elsie was charming. Tommy's wife was a divorcee from a fancy family and she said that if Elsie made clothes like they looked on her she'd make a fortune in Frisco. She said, "You boys can have your theatre; I'll take Elsie any day." They laughed a lot.

"What were you and Tommy talking about before we left?"

"You mostly. Tommy thinks you're rich. Are you?"

"I wish I were."

"Tommy asked what was in it for me. I told him that I loved you."

"Darling."

"He said love wasn't enough. What is in it, mom? Where do we go from here?"

"Must we go somewhere?"

"I have to. I'm not even your boy-friend in this place. I'm nothing."

"You're everything to me."

"Then let's pull out of here, mom, together, shall we? You heard what Tommy's wife said. She wasn't joking . . . she'd set you up in Frisco. You got a golden touch anyway. So what are you afraid of?"

"Gardenia's been awfully good to me, Larry. And a bird in the hand is worth . . ."

"A nest egg."

"The nest egg's for you, darling."

"And you sit on it. What do I get out of it? Shirts . . . a suit . . . a car . . . in your name."

"It was your idea to put it in my name."

"And you kissed me for it. Why don't you give me something in my name now . . . when I want it? Did it ever occur to you that my future's kind of shaky when I've got nothing to go by but what you say? I don't mind your lying . . ."

"Lying!"

"Yeah, I kind of like it some of the time. But not now. I didn't come with you for your money, mom . . ."

"I know, darling."

"But you're so goddam tight and cagey you make me want it. Did it ever occur to you what would happen to me if you conked out?"

"I wouldn't care what happened to me if you weren't here, darling."

"It's easy to say. It doesn't prove a thing. But you can prove it in another way."

"Larry, even if I could get the ten thousand you want, then what? You'd leave me."

"Why? You'd come to Frisco every weekend. I could come here. Only I don't want ten anymore. I want twenty-five."

"Twenty-five thousand? From where would I get so much money?"

"Jesus, you're mean. You've got it."

"Where, I'd like to know."

"In the bank. Not this one, in Jackson."

"You broke open my drawer!"

"No, I picked it."

"Oh Larry, how could you? I trusted you."

"Yeah, not enough to let me see your bank account, that's for sure."

"But to go into my private papers . . ."

"What did you expect me to do when you're fitting all the time? Think about you? Well, I'll tell you something nice, mom: I did think about you . . . a lot. Now think about me a little."

"Twenty-five thousand isn't little. What would you do with it, Larry. Leave me?"

"You've got leaving on the brain. Who said I was leaving you? We can get married in Frisco. Giovanni's hard to spell but it's easier than Wojevec. But if you want me I cost twenty-five grand in cash, in sacred or profane love, any way you want it, mom. It's no hold up. I could go downstairs this minute and tell Delia I'm not your son, but I'm no rat. You're smart, mom, you knew that when you brought me home. No, twenty-five, considering what you've got, it's about fair."

"But you don't need that much for Tommy"

"Tommy or no Tommy, mom, twenty-five in cash."

"But it takes time to get cash."

"It takes time to talk too. Don't prolong the agony, mom. It's too painful . . . for you. Because what you love isn't me, mom, it's money . . ."

"Oh, darling . . ."

"Then here's the phone. Call the bank in Jackson. I'll hold your hand. I'll always hold your hand."

"What'll I tell them?"

"Tell them the truth: that your son and lover wants to make an investment. No, I guess you can't say that but why do you have to say anything? Tell them to wire it today so that we can get it to-morrow."

That was on Thursday. Friday morning Elsie said that she was too busy to go to Frisco for the weekend, that after she got the money Larry should go alone. She wanted him to think that she trusted him.

"If you'll deliver the dresses, darling, after you've dropped me at the bank, I can walk home."

"With all that cash on you, won't you be nervous?"

"I shouldn't be, darling; you'll be going so much further with it."

"On my way back I'll drive by just in case."

He missed her at the bank but he saw her walking. He felt very gay. She didn't see him so he played cops and robbers. "Bang, bang, bang." She jumped.

"Darling."

"Got it?"

She nodded.

"Where?"

"Here." She patted her bosom.

Upstairs Elsie took out the bills but she took a long time doing it. "It's hard for me, darling. Not because I wouldn't give you everything I have, but you don't understand how poor I was. My mother was an invalid and I worked to take care of her, all the time. It's true, darling. I never had anything I wanted until I had you . . . and my son, of course. The truth is, even if you don't believe it, that I didn't know any money had been left me until after my mother died. I never knew my father. Now that I'm telling you this I might as well tell you every-thing : I'm not even sure my mother was married."

"We've a lot in common. I'm a bastard too. Only my dad didn't leave me a hundred grand. I've been really modest, mom. I didn't ask you to split it. You got more in there?"

"No."

"Where's the rest?"

"They didn't have more cash and you said ten thousand for . . ."

"You know what I said. Christ, I'm getting out of here."

"Larry, dearest. Listen . . ."

"Get away from me. You're so tight you couldn't give it away until you met me. That story about your son. Jesus Christ, did you think I was never with a woman? Immaculate Conception No. 2. I'll say this for you: you saved it for your son. That's more than Mary did. Can I have your suitcase or should I go down and ask Delia for a paper bag?"

"Larry, stop. I'll give you the rest. I want to. It's just that to put so much money like that in a theatre is so different from what I believe in."

"You believe in money period. Leave your hands out of there . . . and let go that suit."

"I will not let go."

"Oh yes you will." He hit her but he hadn't meant to hit so hard. She fell against the mantel and folded. Her head must have struck the corner. There was a tiny bit of blood. He couldn't get a heart beat.

"Oh God, mom. I could have waited. You waited for me so long, and I loved you too, you crazy, stupid liar. Why did it go wrong?"

When George came home on Friday he thought he heard voices upstairs in Elsie's rooms, like a quarrel, but they stopped all of a sudden. He didn't mention it to Delia because she was so touchy whenever he said anything about noises from up there. Sometimes, not always, they saw Elsie and Larry when they went out in the evening, but that night they didn't see them. Sunday morning Delia guessed they'd gone off for the weekend although she thought it was funny Elsie hadn't told her. She didn't go upstairs because since Larry was there she felt it was kind of intruding-like. But early Monday morning, when they weren't back, she went up and then the phone rang. It was the police down at Oakdale. They said Elsie's car with the keys in it had been at the Oakdale station since Friday, and then he heard Delia screaming. He ran up and there she was crying and rocking Elsie in her arms. She shouldn't have touched the body like that but she was always crazy about Elsie. George thought it was because Delia had never had a child of her own that she had taken to Elsie on account of her devotion to Larry. To the first Larry, the real Larry. Of course with Delia so broken-hearted what was the sense making her feel worse by saying all over again about the something rotten in Denmark? All he ever said, trying to comfort her, was, "Aren't you glad you never had a son?"

A Family Affair

"How long has he been on the phone?" Millicent asked.

Paul looked at his watch. "About twenty minutes."

"That's quite a call from Chicago."

"I'll bet he won't come."

"Where!?" Millicent asked. The word exploded. She was small and violent. It was part of her attraction.

They were sitting in the foyer of the Schwarzenburg Palais Hotel. They had come to Vienna to meet Jaimie and then go on to the wonderful part of the vacation, in this girl's, Eloise Smith's boat. They didn't know the girl but they had no doubt that she was both strange and charming, for they knew Jaimie's girls, and they had little doubt either that she would think he was hers while they knew he was theirs, for Jaimie, in Paul's phrase, didn't "attach solid". They always wondered why and used to talk about it, often with Jaimie but more often without, until once Paul said, "I think you're too interested, Millicent." "I like that," she had said, "You're basically in love with him." Which was silly, pseudo-psychological claptrap, for the fact was that they both loved him.

The trip had seemed a natural for all kinds of reasons: the girl with the boat, it wasn't exactly a yacht but a felucca, whatever that was, and the girl was part Greek and knew the isles like the palm of her hand. Then too they had never been in Vienna and Jaimie, who'd been there for over a year, had friends and, from his point of view, it was timed perfectly. He had finished his work with his homeopathic doctor and also an article about him called *A Kick in Heaven*, the title from a street oddly named Ein Stoss in Himmel: he was hipped on it, not only the name but on homeopathy and on his doctor in particular, who he said was a genius. But everything went wrong. First the girl had delayed the trip, engine trouble she had cabled, and then the night

85

of their arrival Paul had been taken ill. Apparently he had almost died from a strange kind of shellfish poisoning, angioneurotic edema it was called, and Millicent thought she'd lose her mind when Jaimie brought in his homeopath. "Either you believe in it or you don't", he had said. Which was very nice, but what did she know about fringe medicine? The man was decent, though, for he'd offered to call in someone else although he said it was unnecessary, and he explained that homeopathy, when successful, at first sometimes aggravated symptoms, and he not only confirmed Jaimie's diagnosis but also the medication and added that if he hadn't acted promptly, it might have been too late. After the gagging was over, Paul's first words to Jaimie were, "You son-of-a-bitch, did you have to goddam near kill me to prove your medicine?" Well, he had proved it. Paul recovered almost as fast as he'd been taken ill, and now . . .

"You can't mean that he . . ." Millicent went on and then Jaimie came in. He didn't look happy.

"How's your father?"

"Not very well."

"Is he worse?"

"It seems so."

"Paul says you won't go with us."

Jaimie looked at them. "He's right. But you can go anyway."

"With a girl we don't know?" Millicent said. "She'd be crazy to see us."

"I'm sorrier than you are."

"Look," Millicent said, "I was born on Viertestrasse. We didn't have the money to fly all over the place. And I liked my father better, from what I hear, than you like yours. But when he was dying I stayed in California with Paul."

"You talk as if it were something to be proud of," Paul said.

"I don't care about the goddam trip."

"That's not true, Millicent," Paul said.

"All right, I do care. But I care about Jaimie more. Every time his family winces he goes home. I don't get it. Everybody has to die."

"Is he dying?" Paul asked.

"I don't know."

"Then it's crazy, Jaimie. After all we did come all the way from California."

86

"That's not nice, Millicent," Paul said.

"But really why? Honestly at thirty-five it's not normal the way you go home. Is it on account of money?"

"No. As a matter of fact they've never been free with money, that is, with me anyway."

"You live pretty well."

"I have a little from my grandfather."

"What is it then?"

"I'll tell you." Jaimie sat down. "I had a little sister, Susie . . . I was seven and she was three . . ."

"I never knew that," Paul said.

"My God," Millicent said, "That was how many years ago?"

"Shut up, Millicent."

"It was at the country club. Paul was there once. It was a golf club really but they had good tennis courts. And an instructor. I was supposed to be very good at tennis. I had a lesson. It was Sunday, after lunch, very hot and no one was there."

"Where were your family?"

"Mother was playing bridge at the club and my father was in a golf tournament. I went out with Susie and our nurse. Her name was Molly Brady. The instructor was late and Molly said she had to go to the bathroom, that I was to keep an eye on Susie. I just loved her. She was gentle and sweet and terribly bright. She had begun to read . . . from being with me, I suppose. She was impish too. She couldn't really hold the racket and when I hit the balls she'd run after them. They were new balls and I was very proud of them. Then she got bored and . . ."

"Where was Molly? With the tennis instructor?"

"How could he know that, Millicent?"

"Didn't your parents bother to know what Molly was like?"

"Anyway, Susie began picking clover at the back of the courts. There was a wire net around them. After a while I banged a ball over the net and went to get it. I wanted Susie to come but she wouldn't. I watched her but I couldn't find the ball. The courts were next to the main road, Sheridan Road, it was almost a highway . . ."

"I can't bear it," Millicent said.

"As I said they were closed in with a steel net and there was an underpass from the main club to the golf course. There was an embankment with a hedge that shielded the club from the road but nobody ever went there. But Susie got out and through the hedge . . . and then it was all over. I remember my parents coming before Molly did because when she came she started screaming, "You're a bad boy, you're a . . ."

"But you don't mean that because of what Molly . . ." Millicent began.

"It wasn't only Molly. Later I overheard my parents when someone asked, 'When it happened, where were you?' and then, 'Where was Jaimie?' and my father said, 'He should have been watching her.' "

"While he was playing golf and your mother bridge," Millicent said. "Jesus, I think it was better on Viertestrasse."

"Gee, Jaimie," Paul said. "All the time I've known you and I didn't know this."

"But didn't your parents, with all that money, have the sense to find someone?" Millicent said. "A psychiatrist or something. It's unbelievable. Didn't you ever have any help?"

"Oh, everybody's had help. It turned out later, when I went to someone, I didn't really need it. Sure, after the accident, I could have used it. I didn't eat and wouldn't speak and I wouldn't go to school and so, after a while, they sent me to boarding school. I don't think my father ever forgave me."

"Forgave." Millicent said. "A little boy of seven."

"Oh he never said anything, but he never really liked me after that. He couldn't help himself, maybe; he'd loved Susie too. After that, so far as I could see, all he did was work. He was always at the office."

"He probably had a girl."

Paul laughed. "You don't know Jaimie's father."

"I think it was then that he became so successful. Anyway he had it easier than my mother. She attached herself to me or tried to, which I suppose is the other side of the metal."

"The worse side," Millicent said. "One thing's for sure. If that had happened to me, I'd have left home."

"You left anyway," Paul said.

"Jaimie still can. Why don't you, Jaimie?"

"You just want to go on that boat, Millicent."

"It's a kind of duty, isn't it, like any other? If Susie had lived, she'd probably have been home more than I ever was. Why shouldn't I go, until I have my own family anyway, when they're in trouble?"

"Because they're always in trouble," Millicent said. "How many times since I've known you have your parents been in the hospital?"

"It's a little incestuous," Paul said.

"Why? I don't go because I'm so fond of them. I don't even like it there. It's all show."

"I mean on account of Susie. Isn't it really for love of her that you still go back? I'll bet that's why you don't ever fall in love."

"It could be."

"I still thing it's childish to keep going home," Millicent said.

"Maybe it mature. It's generous," Paul said. "When do you go?"

"Now."

The private wing, the same floor, the same flowers along the wall stacked for the night, at the end of the corridor the same suite. Jaimie opened the door. In the anteroom more flowers and a nurse who looked up.

"I'm his son," Jaimie said and put down his bag. "How is he?"

"Comfortable. He's very tired."

"I won't disturb him."

"Oh there's someone in there anyway."

His father was motionless, staring at the ceiling, and beside him, holding his hand as if it belonged to her, was Gillian Bowman.

Jaimie remembered Gillian from the time when she had first come into his father's office. He was a boy then but he'd been crazy about her because she was so young and pretty and quick and friendly too, and also there was something different about her, for unlike the other girls she was almost part of the firm. This was because when her Aunt Kate Bowman, who for years had been his father's secretary, was promoted to bookkeeper, she had brought Gillian in as secretary for one of the junior partners. Jaimie remembered that his father was so fond of Gillian – he had great respect for the Bowman competence in any case – that he'd thought of switching her to his. But then, suddenly, Gillian married. All Jaimie ever knew was that she married a man named Sommers who had been in the war and been wounded and was supposedly somehow so well connected in the east that Jaimie's mother invited them to dinner. But the marriage didn't work out.

Sommers was a drinker and a bad one; he beat up Gillian. As they were both Catholic Jaimie's father couldn't get her a divorce but he arranged a separation and then for some reason Gillian didn't go back in the firm.

Could it possibly be that his father and Gillian . . .? Why the old bastard. Jaimie felt like a little boy confronted with the facts of life, for it was almost beyond belief that his correct father had been so devious and free, but his astonishment was mixed with something close to admiration, for Gillian, in spite of the years, with her raven hair and lovely skin, was still very beautiful.

Gillian saw him and let go the hand and her smile said the pleasure she hoped Jaimie might bring. "Look who's here, Mr. Hoch."

His father turned his head. "Jaimie."

"Have they got you down again, father?" Jaimie said, taking his hand . . . and pulse. "How are you?"

"I'm still here."

"You look better than that." It was not true. His father had the stale color of fear.

"I'll leave you two gentlemen," Gillian said and stood up. She was expensively dressed but missed elegance which suited her fine. There was no doubt about it : she was a wonder.

"I wish you wouldn't go," Jaimie said. "I want to talk to you."

"Me?" Gillian said and sat down again.

"When did you get here?" his father asked.

"Just now. I came from the airport."

"Haven't you seen your mother?"

"I'll go home afterwards."

"She'll be waiting for you. This has been very hard on her, Jaimie."

"What about you?"

His father shook his head, meaning words couldn't tell how hard. "Why do you want to see Gillian?"

"Why wouldn't I? You haven't changed, Gillian."

"Oh, come on."

"Did you know that when I was thirteen I was in love with you? I wrote poems to you . . .

Gillian with her lovely smile,
It's like the Nile, it doth beguile.

> Gillian with her coal black hair,
> It's like a dare . . .

and so on."

Gillian laughed and his father tried to. "You didn't ask Gillian to stay to recite poetry, did you?"

"I wanted to ask her to help me give you my medicine, that is of course, if you'll take it. It can be very healing."

"What kind of medicine is it?" Gillian asked.

"Homeopathic."

"Oh, the magic of the minimum dose."

"How do you know?"

"Aunt Kate used to cure us with those little pills. They can do wonders, Mr. Hoch."

"Why don't you try it this time, father?"

"I'll try anything."

"Then we might as well begin now." Jaimie took a bottle from his pocket and poured two drops of liquid on the back of his father's hand. "Lick it, it won't hurt you." He took out two more bottles. "Here are your pills, Gillian."

"Do you use them all?"

"You rotate them. The important thing is that they're given regularly . . . every fifteen minutes or so around the clock."

"For how long?" his father asked.

"Until you're better."

"You look better already, Mr. Hoch."

Jaimie put the bottles in the drawer of the bedside table. "I keep the last dose in back so as not to get mixed up, also so the doctors won't see them. When there's a nurse around it means a little sleight of hand but it's surprising what they don't see."

Jaimie's father had dozed off. "What about when he's asleep?"

Jaimie took a tablet from the front bottle. "Open your mouth, father . . . and let it dissolve," he said in a low voice. "He needn't wake up. I've shown so many people, parents mostly, sometimes I wonder if it's the medication or the assurance that the constant attention . . . every few minutes all through the night . . . gives the child." He looked at his father. "Still I have reason to believe it's also the medicine."

"But you can't do it alone, Jaimie."

"I forgot to ask you the main thing. Will you spell me?"

"You know I will."

"I'll do the nights . . . won't that be better for you? . . . only if you could possibly stay for the next two hours, then I could go home."

"I can stay as long as you want."

"Actually we should have another person. Eight hours is about all one can take. I'm trained for more, but even so."

"What about Emily?" his father said without opening his eyes.

"Who's Emily?"

"My daughter. She and your father are great friends." Gillian went to the door. "I must telephone her I'll be late. When would you want her?"

"Whenever she can come. How old is she?"

"Twenty-one, almost," Gillian said and went out.

Jaimie's father opened his eyes. "She may be tired. She's had a long trip."

"From where?"

"Bennington. She's at college."

"If it's her vacation, she won't want to spend it here."

"She may. She's a fine girl, remarkable, in fact, considering her father."

"Sommers?"

"Yes. She has none of his shortcomings. She's intelligent, dependable and lovely."

Gillian came back. "Em'll be here at eight."

Jaimie put a tablet in his father's mouth. "Every fifteen minutes. I'll be back as soon as I can."

"Jaimie!" his mother said, kissing him. "What took you so long, dear? I waited dinner for you."

"That was nice of you. I thought you'd have eaten. Go ahead, I have to wash."

"I can't tell Frieda to wait any longer, Jaimie."

When he came back his mother was at the table. "Where's your luggage?"

"At the hospital. I'm going to sleep there."

"Why? Do you think your father's so ill?" and his mother began to cry.

"You said he was when you phoned." Jaimie put his fork down. "I came to see him in any case. And you too of course, but he's the one who needs help."

"I need it too, Jaimie. I've been very lonely these last months."

"Poor mother."

"How do you think your father really is?"

"Not very well. I brought him some medicine."

"You can ask Dr. Guthrie in the morning what he thinks of it. He's so devoted to your father that he'd do anything in the world for him."

"Anything to his advantage."

"You mean money?"

"Or esteem. He's an operator, mother. My medicine's homeopathic."

"He probably doesn't believe in it."

"Do you think he can believe in his with father back in hospital . . . for how many times? Anyway it doesn't make any difference what he believes in: father's taking mine."

"You don't mean you're giving your father something without consulting Dr. Guthrie? I never heard of such a thing. What if something happened to him?"

"Who would know?"

"But if he . . . but if there was an . . . a . . . autopsy?"

"He has to be dead first."

"Jaimie! How can you even think such a thing?"

"What I think is that he'll be all right."

"How can you take such a risk?"

"Doctors do all the time or decent ones do. What do you think happened before abortion was legal? Every time a doctor referred a girl somewhere he risked losing his licence. Think of that."

"I don't see what abortion has to do with it except that it's unethical and what you're doing is too."

"I don't know that curing's unethical."

"Are you so sure you can cure him?"

"It's worth the try. But let's not argue, mother."

"Why don't you eat, Jaimie?" His mother sighed. "And you can still see Dr. Guthrie tomorrow and . . ."

"I saw him when I left the hospital. He was with Beare. In fact they were talking about father."

"What did they say?"

"Beare's a surgeon. What do you think?"

"You don't mean they're thinking of operating?" and his mother began to cry again.

"Not if I can help it. Beare's a bastard."

"He's the best surgeon in Chicago."

"Well, make up your mind," Jaimie said and began to eat. "What happened to your hair?"

"Why? Is anything the matter with it?"

"No, I'm not used to it so blue, that's all . . . And how are you, really, mother?"

"You mean my health? It's all right. You know, Jaimie, when men reach a certain age they often become foolish about younger women."

"What age, mother?"

"Well, I'm talking about your father. He's always been fond of Gillian Bowman and we all know how helpful he's been to her through the years, but whenever he's ill he likes her to come to the hospital and lately she comes every day and he's not supposed to have visitors."

Jaimie looked at his mother. "Are you jealous?"

"Jealous! Of course I'm not jealous."

"Then what difference does it make?"

"It makes a difference to me. The doctors limit my visits to once a day and then for only half an hour . . . as if I could do him any harm," and again his mother began to cry.

"If you cry all the time, you probably upset him."

"Well, Gillian upsets me. It's my right to be there, isn't it, not hers?"

"Yes, it is but it's the wrong time. He's an old man seriously ill and he likes her company. He seems fond of her daughter too. I didn't know she had one."

"Emily."

"What's she like?"

"I haven't seen her in years. But I hear about her now and then. You remember Rue Thorpe? Her daughter, Frances, goes to college with Emily . . . I've forgotten where."

"Bennington."

"How do you know?"

"Father told me."

"You're better informed than I am. Rue says she's very charming but reserved. Apparently she doesn't run around the way so many girls do today. As a child she was very lovely, I must say, not at all like Gillian; there was something almost patrician about her, probably from her father. You know, I never altogether believed that story about his drinking. Oh, certainly he drank but it could be that he was driven to it. There are always two sides to these things. Under the veneer she's gross. And it's very inconsiderate of me, her making a public show of herself. I can't understand you, Jaimie. Don't you think really I ought to do something about her being there so much?"

"It's a little late in the day."

"What do you mean by that? Surely not that there's anything between them?"

"How should I know? You're married to him, I'm not. But why pick on Gillian? Obviously it's father who wants her there."

"I'm not interested in who wants what. I want to know what I should do about it."

"Accept it."

"And the doctors? What do you suppose they think?"

"What do you care?" Jaimie got up. "But then you always did care more about what people think than anything else."

"You certainly don't love me if you say a thing like that. How can you even think it?"

"You have no compassion."

"I never heard of such a thing. I'm filled with compassion . . . When will you be back?"

"In the morning. Shall I call you?"

"I have compassion for your father's health. I worry so I don't sleep at night. So don't call me too early."

Jaimie's father opened his eyes. "You've had dinner and heard everything your mother had to say and back so soon? What time is it?"

"Almost three."

Jaimie's father smiled. "What's in that stuff? I feel better than since I don't know when. I want to talk to you, Jaimie, about money among other things. What I want to tell you doesn't only concern you.

It's in the nature of a confidence. It'll take a little explaining."

"Why don't you tell me another time?" He gave his father a tablet.

"What if something happened? If my ticker didn't hold out?"

"Your ticker's fine." Jaimie took his father's pulse. "I wouldn't worry. Sleep now if you can."

Although Jaimie had not spent the night imagining what Emily would be like, he was more curious, for a daughter of Gillian, if for no other reason, should be special. On the other hand her report was suspect, because he had met girls whom his parents had praised before, and he pictured her in debutante blue with bangles. Her coming there could mean anything, that she was obedient and kind or ambitious and scheming, for after all her mother's patron was a rich man supposedly headed for the last round-up.

"Uncle Edgar, am I too early?"

Well, she was special all right. She was small and fine, with her auburn hair cropped close, showing shell-like ears waiting for something . . . music perhaps. She was very pale and her eyes, more green than blue, reminded Jaimie of someone he couldn't place. They were intelligent eyes and kept shifting, nervously taking everything in. There was something incredibly sweet about her . . . maybe it was her voice. She was no debutante, that was for sure. She wore an off-blue blouse with almost matching stockings and a dark purplish brown skirt and she'd taken off her scarf; it was lime green and in her hand. From the colors Jaimie wondered if she painted. She walked toward his father on high-heeled lizard shoes, the one incongruous item in her get-up; in spite of them she walked like a dancer. What she saw must have pleased her for her smile opened enough for a sound to come out like a little gasp for pleasure.

"You don't look sick, Uncle Edgar." She kissed him on the forehead. "You look fine. Is it the new medicine?"

"Perhaps I am now that you're here, Em." He took her hand and patted it.

They seemed more intimate than Gillian's "great friends" had indicated but what made Jaimie marvel was how affectionate his father could be.

"Did you have a good trip? And how are you, dear?"

"I'm all right, but the doctor must be tired." She looked at Jaimie. "Aren't you? That's why I came so early."

"I was, but I'm awake now."

"You won't have to stay awake long . . . if you'll show me the medicine and how to give them. Although, truly, Uncle Edgar doesn't look as if he needs them. I'm sorry I go on talking. I'd planned not to say a word but you've made me nervous."

"Why?"

"I suppose because Gillian made you out such a paragon. I hope it's not serious," and she laughed. "Truly, though, I never heard her speak that way about anyone. She said you'd done a miracle with Uncle Edgar. He was so much better last night when she left. I'm to call her as soon as I can. But I go on and on. I'm sorry."

"Do you want to call her now?" Jaimie's father asked.

"It's a good idea," Jaimie said. He took the bottles from the drawer and put the drops on his father's hand. "That's how it's done. I'll show these to Emily in the other room and send the nurse in."

"Are you still nervous?"

"No."

"Should I show you the dosages or do you want to phone first?"

"It doesn't make any difference."

"Well, you just give the tablets one after the other and then the drops again. That's all there is to it. You rotate them."

"Every fifteen minutes?" She looked at him straight on, no eye shifting.

"How do you know?"

"Gillian told me. What do we do, though, when I'm not here?"

"Won't Gillian be here?" He gave her the bottles. He wanted to take her hand but he didn't. She didn't draw her hand away, though.

"She'll come this afternoon at two and stay until ten. We want you to have some rest. But I'm supposed to walk for an hour between eleven and twelve."

"When my mother's here, you mean."

"Oh is that it. I thought I'd put one of each pill in the front of the drawer where your father can reach them. What do you think?"

"That's what I think." Although he'd never seen anything like her, he had the feeling that he'd known her before or should have. He so wanted to touch her that he was dizzy and it wasn't fatigue. "Where will you walk?"

"Along the lake. It's nice this time of year."

"Isn't it dangerous?"

"Oh no, not in the daytime. There's almost no one there."

"I think there'll be someone there."

It was nippy on the lake front. There was no one on the promenade. At the park end the spray came over the walk. Then the green scarf showed and she came out from the underpass.

"You must be exhausted."

"I'm happy."

He took her hand and they walked toward the park. He was more than happy, he was content, a feeling that he'd never had before and he sensed that she felt it too. They said nothing. Then she laughed.

"Don't you talk?"

"I can."

"Is it because you're afraid that if I start, I won't stop, like this morning?"

"No. I like to hear you talk. I like it either way. What shall we talk about?"

"You."

"Let's begin with you. Are you a painter?"

"I'm not anything. But you win anyway. I wanted to be a sculptor."

"You talk as if it were all over. Aren't there good people at Bennington?"

"But they don't teach. It's not their fault, I suppose. Bennington's a social place. What I should do, if I were really serious, is to work in somebody's studio."

"Will you?"

She looked at him. "I may."

They crossed over to the park.

"Did you ever hear of Kirsta?"

"No."

"He's very good. He left last term. He wanted to take me but Gillian was against it."

"Why? Does she know about sculpture?"

"She's so protective. She wants me to graduate before I do anything else. And she's not innocent, as I suppose you know. Kirsta doesn't want me just to sculpt."

"Is it difficult with a mother like Gillian?"

"Because she's so beautiful?"

"On that score you don't have to worry."

"It's difficult because she treats me like a princess. She wasn't, as I suppose you know. She had a hard beginning. She was very poor, Aunt Kate supported them. Her father, like mine, left them. She wants me to have 'all the advantages she didn't have'. And I have, thanks to your father too. What I resent is why she doesn't come out with it, for God's sake? Does she think I don't know what their relationship is, or was?"

"Why don't you come out with it and ask her?"

"Oh, if she wants to pretend, it's her right to, I suppose. Why make her unhappy? I love her enough for that. But it's belittling."

They'd come to the Lincoln statue.

"Do you like him?"

"Who? Lincoln or your father?"

"Both."

She studied Lincoln. "Yes, I like him. If you do one good thing, it's enough, isn't it?"

"And my father?"

"I used to love him when I was little. He was the only father I knew."

"You must have reminded him of my sister. You know about her?"

"Yes."

"You remind me of her too. I feel almost as if you belong to me. It's strange; I felt it from the beginning. Or maybe belong's the wrong word. People shouldn't belong to each other."

"I wish they did," she said and kissed him. "I've got to go back."

They crossed over from the park.

"I didn't like Uncle Edgar today, though."

"You were awfully sweet to him."

"Well, he's sick. But he was so mean to you when I said it must have been your medicine."

"He was overcome with your presence. So am I."

"It's so ungrateful."

"He's never been generous with me."

"How do you know so much about homeopathy?"

"I don't. I studied with a doctor for a year in Vienna, but to do it right I ought to work in a hospital somewhere, in Stuttgart maybe."

"You talk as if it were all over."

"It's the doctor who prescibed. I told him father's symptoms. I'm to telephone him every day . . . I'm loaded with medicines . . . and as the symptoms change he'll tell me what to give. It's very precise. I suppose that's why most doctors ignore it . . . it takes so much time. It would be better if my doctor came, of course, but there's no point if father won't see him."

"Maybe he won't have to."

Jaimie stopped walking.

"Aren't you coming the rest of the way?"

"It's better if I don't."

"Why?"

"I'll tell you at lunch, that is, if you'll have lunch with me."

"Where?"

"The Whitehall's near. There'll be nobody there after two. Is two fifteen all right?"

"No. I don't want to leave you."

"I don't want to leave you, ever," and he walked a little further but not all the way.

"Am I late?"

"No, I'm early. Gillian was early."

"How'd it go?"

"You've cured him. Gillian thinks so too. Why are we in the elevator?" Then she saw the key.

Jaimie opened the door. There was a table with anemones and through a second door, in the bedroom, more flowers. The table was set with covered dishes, salad in a bowl, something on a side table and wine in a bucket. Next to one place, hers surely, was a little box tied with a string.

He kissed her but she didn't respond. She wasn't surprised by the embrace but by the room.

"Are you hungry?"

"I should be now that you've gone to all this trouble." She took off a plate lid. "Oh, jellied trout, my favourite." It was the first sign of real pleasure. There was something wrong.

He poured the wine.

"What are you thinking about?"

Her eyes took in the room. "I'm not used to this . . . movie set."

"Is it as bad at that?"

He kissed her cheek and they sat down. She shook the little box. "Diamonds, I hope."

"Yep."

But she didn't open it. They didn't talk for a while. Then he asked, "Is anything the matter?"

"I shouldn't say." But she said it anyway. "Are you married?"

"I'd like to be."

"Then why the secrecy?" The sadness evaporated. She was all smiles.

"Oh darling." He got up and kissed her and this time she put her arms around him.

"I don't want my family to know anything because they always spoil everything. I don't say it's intentional, but they never miss. It may be very infantile of me to let them, I don't know. My friend's wife in Vienna thought so. We were all set to go to Greece."

"Have they ever spoiled it with a girl?"

"Yes."

"Tell me about her."

He looked at her. "There's only one girl to tell about and they aren't going to spoil it with her because they won't get the chance. It may sound silly or intuitive or superstitious, but believe me. Does Gillian know you're here?"

"No. I guess I wanted it secret too. In a way, though, it's a shame she doesn't. You're everything she's always wanted for me. Or am I ahead of you?"

"No," and he took her hand. "You're with me."

"Then I'll open the diamonds."

"They're about the only diamonds you'll have, Em. I have no real money of my own."

"I have. Or I will have soon. My father left me a trust fund. It's supposed to be a lot . . . Oh, they are diamonds! Oh Jaimie, how lovely. What a beautiful ring."

"My grandfather gave it to my grandmother the day they were married. You see I am intuitive. If you're an heiress, I didn't want to monkey around."

"Well, father, how does it feel to be dressed?"
"Better. Where have you been keeping yourself?"
"What time is the car coming?"
"At eleven. You know I had a good mind before leaving to tell Guthrie about your medicine."
"It was better that you didn't. It would only make trouble."
"Sit down, Jaimie. I want to talk to you. By the way, your mother tells me you don't sleep at home, that you've taken a room somewhere. Why's that?"
"I didn't want to . . . for lots of reasons. One is that it's near the hospital. I didn't know you were going to respond to the medicine so quickly, that we could stop the around the clock business so soon. As a matter of fact, I thought you'd go home last week."
"Guthrie thought it more prudent here."
"More convenient surely. You couldn't have had Gillian at home."
"She's very attentive, it's true. But you aren't any more, Jaimie, and Emily neglects me too. She's suddenly become a party girl, Gillian tells me, and doesn't get home until the small hours, until dawn sometimes. Well, she's entitled to a good time, but she hasn't been here since that first day and her vacation's over soon and she knows I'm going home this morning. It's not like her. Do you ever go to parties?"
"What do you want to talk to me about, father?"
"Several things. You're a strange boy, Jaimie. You've never given any indication that you wanted to know about my affairs."
"You've never been open with me."
"Well, I plan to be now. Although I'm a rich man, Jaimie, I won't be here forever. I want you to know something about my will at least. Perhaps you're thinking that through the years I haven't been very generous with you."
"With money, you mean?"
"What else?"
"There's also affection, father."
"Well, I'm talking about money. After your schooling I didn't give

you anything because it wasn't indicated. You had your grandfather's estate, it wasn't large but it made you independent."

"He loved me."

"Why do you alway get off the main issue? It's very irritating. What I'm trying to tell you, and I should think you'd be interested, is that when I die the bulk of my estate will go to you. Naturally your mother during her lifetime will have most of the income but . . . why do you smile?"

"Do I? I don't feel like it. You can never give me anything outright, can you?"

"Are you asking for something? If you are, I'll certainly consider it. I'm not unmindful of how helpful your medicine has been."

"I'm not asking to be paid, father . . . or are you thanking me?"

"In a way, certainly, but you're making it very difficult for me because there's something else I want to tell you that you should know. Emily has a substantial trust fund and you're a trustee."

"I am? Why?"

"I made you one."

"But her father made the trust."

"I'm her father."

Jaimie got up and went to the window and looked out into a grey bleak world.

"Does that shock you? Don't judge your father too harshly. I was a broken man when your sister died."

"And you found consolation."

"Not immediately. But then Gillian came along, and one thing led to another. I found great comfort in Emily, it's true."

"And mother? Who comforted her? Or did she have a lover too?"

"Your mother's an exceptional woman. She has great self-esteem and I've always respected it. I thought it kinder not to let her know. Believe me, it hasn't been easy, but I've taken every precaution to protect her."

"Protect her!? You protected yourself. I was brought up to respect you but so help me God I don't know why. Did you ever think of protecting Emily whom you're so fond of?"

"You take this out of all proportion. I've just been telling you what I've done to protect Emily with a trust fund."

"Dear God, is that honestly all you can think about? I'm not a statue. Did it ever cross your mind that there might be some attraction?"

"Has there been? You frighten me."

"About what? What would you care if it didn't affect your immediate welfare? You and mother are pretty well suited after all. Neither of you has ever given a thought to anything but yourselves. That's the reason why she doesn't know about Gillian . . . or Emily."

"What is?"

"Because she thinks of herself, not you. Did either of you ever think of me when I was a little boy and Susie was killed? And you think of Emily . . . with a trust fund. Jesus Christ."

"Where are you going?"

"I don't know, father."

"Jaimie! You're so pale. What's the matter, darling?"

"Let's get out of here, Em. Let's go now."

"Where?"

"Anywhere. But now."

"All right. Where have you been? Your hair's all wet."

"Along the lake."

"Without me? Why? Did you see your father?"

"Oh, Em, don't leave me."

"Why would I leave you, Jaimie? Did your father say something?"

"Yes."

"Does he know we're married?"

"No."

"Even if he did, he couldn't do anything about it. How can he upset you so, Jaimie?"

He pulled her down next to him. "Oh, Em. You know, at different times there were different customs. In Egypt, the Pharaohs . . ."

"What is it, Jaimie?"

"And now, with over-population, customs are changing even more. And anyway what do we really know about what happens in people's private lives . . ."

"You're not going to lose me. What did your father say?"

"He said . . . he's your father."

"You know, I thought so once, and not so long ago. It's funny, when you came along it never occurred to me again." She kissed him.

"I loved you so much, I guess I couldn't think. It explains a lot, doesn't it? That's why we loved each other right away."

"Don't you care?"

"Who will know? Gillian won't tell and certainly your parents won't."

"My mother doesn't even know."

"Well, there you are. What's worrying you, darling?"

Bella Figura

Pamela and I arrived in Rome three years ago with our children, a dream nurse, the promise of a perfect flat and unlimited enthusiasm. But whether love that for some time had been beckoning was quickened by the sight of Roman lovers walking out in the cool of the evening, or whether the continual reading of *Mary Poppins* had greater effect on the reader than on her little listeners, who is ever to say? The fact is, in any case, that on the second night our nurse flew out of the window. Simultaneously the promised flat evaporated into thin air and with it a good part of our enthusiasm. We still had the children.

As the days went by we began to feel, as in a dream, that what was happening couldn't be real. But one awakes from a dream, even if to find the object of all desire gone. Our predicament was in reverse, for our dream – to come abroad and live in Rome – had come true: we were actually there and yet we weren't there at all. To be sure from our hotel at dusk we could see the light turn the ancient buildings into red and gold, we could even touch these buildings as we waited in doorways for dismal agents to show us dismal flats, and sometimes, when it wasn't raining, we drove to the Villa Borghese, the loveliest of all central parks, but not to watch the sun go down over St. Peter's nor to walk in meditation with bearded patriarchs under the pines. We fed the ducks and watched Pulcinella punch Arlecchino. He punched with malice, intent on making the dream a nightmare.

One aspect of our predicament, however, had nothing dreamy about it. On the night of our arrival, due to a misunderstanding, no rooms had been available in the little hotel where we had made reservations, but in their stead the manager, apparently as a great personal favour, had booked me a suite at the Grand Hotel. It consisted of a hall leading to an enormous bath (the only one of the great antique *terme* that we were destined to see for some time), two double rooms, a little salon where our nurse subsequently slept on her last loveless night, and a terrace with a balustrade that even our children couldn't climb. Well, there was that first flush of innocent wild enthusiasm, we were tired, it was for a day or two at most, you only live once, and so on. Now the Grand Hotel is not the Ritz but it is nevertheless the Grand Hotel. The days drifted into a week, the weeks into almost a month, and the bills! We knew that we should get out of the suite and for that matter out of the hotel, and, what's more, that if we didn't there would be no point to looking further at flats. But our ability to act, together with everything else, had disintegrated, and there was always the hope of another day.

That we were still hopeful is a monument to courage, for the tide of battle had gone against us from the start. Without a nurse, naturally we had sallied forth with the children, not altogether innocently either, for we had known all along that Luke, our older, was enormously gifted at "fixing" things, but for some unaccountable reason, until we began house hunting, we had never recognised his incredible speed. Now it so happens that furnished flats in Rome, even the grubbiest of them, are filled with innumerable little porcelain baubles, mostly heirlooms and apparently *all* of perfectly astonishing value. Well, after that disastrous beginning, we re-formed ranks: while I remained with the children, Pamela reconnoitered alone. But this seemingly sensible plan, like others in another cold war, had the drawback of ignorance. We did not know about a *caparra*, a deposit given by a prospective tenant to the landlord. Its amount is at the discretion of the tenant, but if the landlord accepts it, he is bound by law to hold the property for a stipulated period or, in the event that he otherwise rents it, to repay double the amount. As Italians do not view with delight the prospect of paying foreigners anything, a *caparra* is in substance a pound of flesh, while a given word is a sometime thing. We learned eventually, but meanwhile whenever Pamela was shown a flat that was remotely habitable, by the time I was mustered in it too had gone with the wind.

Future historians, reviewing this Roman campaign, will doubtless say that we bungled it, that we had only ourselves to blame, that in a land renowned for its gentle manners our first step should have been to replace our nurse. But our children had been devoted to her and they were also suddenly in an alien world where to have coupled them to a stranger with whom they couldn't communicate would have been the better part of cruelty. Besides, they were in the middle of *Mary Poppins*. Nevertheless we tried, and, as it first appeared, not unsuccessfully. The woman we engaged was attractive, her English, although extremely odd, was fluent, and there seemed no reason to mistrust her fondness for the children. Indeed, in a matter of days, she gave evidence of a maternal passion so intense that we became uneasy. It seemed curious too that in spite of it she would not work nights, that is, with us, and we began to suspect that she was otherwise employed in a profession that, while affording her incidental opportunity to practise English, denied her child-rearing, although of course not acts prerequisite to this supposedly sublime experience. We are not prudes and it may well be that women such as this one, just because they are starved for affection, would make the best nannies. But we had not come to Rome to test this theory and anyway, as has been indicated, Luke had already given sufficient proof of his remarkable precocity.

After this interlude the state of my morale together with the exchequer almost reached the point of no return. I had never been either a solitary or morning drinker, but insomuch as the children might soon be indigent, I hit upon a plan for at least their survival. On a continent where a dry martini is at a premium, I instructed them with patience, love and care. It was not very difficult, for Baby Rachel loved the sound of ice against the glass, they both loved olives and, as Luke explained to his mother, who took a dim view of the proceedings, I was less gloomy and sometimes downright funny when drunk. Besides, for the past ten days it had rained incessantly and there was no place to go.

At this juncture one morning when we were whooping it up, Pamela burst in flushed with victory. She had put down a *caparra* and she said I was to arise – "pull yourself together" were the words – and meet the agent who would be waiting at *Via in Caterina* No. 6, and she handed me a card on which this address was written. I studied it so carefully that Pamela unkindly mistook my concentration for an inability to focus, and said as much and more. With the composure that comes from superior knowledge, I explained that no street in Rome began with the word "in", but she contradicted me, and advised furthermore, in the event that I could walk, not to take any back talk from the cab driver either, for, said she, "Even Romans don't know where it is." "Where then is it?", I asked with suspicion not altogether alcoholic, for there is a modern section of Rome called Parioli, an ambience not unlike Hollywood although less substantial, and agents, in spite of warnings to the contrary, head straight for it every time. *"The Via in Caterina,"* said Pamela a little smugly, "is just beyond the Palazzo Farnese and runs for one block into the *Via Giulia."* At this I jumped up and began to dress, for the *Via Giulia,* as it winds to the Tiber, is a marvel of ancient dark palaces, all reminiscent of glory, love and murder, and was exactly where we had wanted to be. "The agent told me," Pamela continued, "that she had never shown this flat before and I believe her. Apparently she is a friend of the proprietors, British Embassy people who have been suddenly transferred. Anyway, it's brand spanking new and has everything we asked for: a terrace, a fireplace, a kitchen with a frigidaire and decent plumbing. It's charmingly furnished too – oh there are too many gadgets but we can fix that. And by the way, it's on the top floor." This was almost too good to be true, because in *Roma Vecchia* modern additions on top of old buildings are altogether desirable and consequently very hard to find. "And the price?" "About two hundred dollars." "What's the matter with it?" "Actually it's rather expensive because, to tell the truth, it's a little on the small side." This proved to be the understatement of all time, but I was no longer listening and on my way.

Via in Caterina No. 6 was by no means a palace but it was sufficiently beaten up to answer our romantic needs. The agent was waiting in the doorway and this too was auspicious, for Italians are notoriously late. Even the entrance augered well; it was littered with debris and foul with cat smells but, after picking our way to the rear, there was a neat little black and white foyer and a newborn baby elevator, all shining and functional as you please. Or so it seemed. Oddly enough this elevator seldom worked after we moved in, but this comes later. At the time we squeezed in and rode up fine.

The top floor was obviously new and what is called a *condominio,* perhaps ungrammatically, for a *condominio* is a group of persons who jointly buy and utilize a property. In the case of a building, a *condominio* is supposed to regulate things too, such as cats and the elevator. But on the whole it is a happy arrangement for, with the exception of the entrance hall, the apartments are separate, usually in different styles and often, due to the nature of an old roof, on different levels and in any case altogether private. The door we entered was open and inside, in the narrow hall, two men and a woman were polishing or rather repolishing the green tiled floor. This hall, together with what could be seen of the room beyond, was immaculate and so were they. The woman wore a faded rose uniform with the apron crisp and starched, the men were in housecoats, one striped with green and the other with yellow, and, altogether, place and people shone with *bella figura*.

Fare bella figura is more than a phrase, it's a way of life with its suggestion of pride and esteem, and around it, touching it and sometimes even in it is the Italian queen bee herself, elegance. The two men, who were both young, pleasant and handsome, stood up, smiled and, with proper *bella figura*, gave way about one foot each. The woman's *bella figura* was of course more obsequious, for after all Mediterranean culture is essentially Arabic. She only faintly smiled and then, leaving the field of honour to the males, took herself off, probably to the kitchen. No birddog was needed to point the scent to first-rate servants and I asked the agent if the people came with the place. "Oh no," she said. It was then, in a land of miracles, that I too had a visitation. I said I would take the flat, sight unseen, if two or even one of the people came with it.

"I don't think it will be possible," the agent said, and she told me that both the men and the woman, among others, had worked for Mr. and Mrs. Osborne, the illustrious owners, who had of course never lived in this little flat but in a very grand establishment and who had, before leaving, placed their several servants elsewhere. She then explained that *persone per bene* would never leave town without first finding work for their *personale*, a feudal custom doubtless kept alive by Italy's long history of poverty. "But just for that reason," said she, "finding good servants in Rome is no problem." Her logic seemed opportune if not downright faulty and I looked doubtful. "In any case," she said, "I will ask them for you. But let's look at the flat first."

We had not gone far – there was not far to go – when I realized that "a little on the small side" had been the words of a woman in despair. It was a doll's house and I mean *doll's*. The master bedroom was eight feet square and completely filled with a huge bed covered in pink brocade. From the headboard gilded cupids peeked out thinking apparently what I was thinking. The "girls' " rooms – subsequently the children's – were eight by four. There were two little drawing rooms, a duplex arrangement, the upper on terrace level and ideal for a discreet gentleman-in-waiting. It was all to be sure charming, but there were no closets, no maid's room and hence no place for a nurse, if and when. But there was one feature that caught my eye. The terrace was likewise on two levels and the upper half had been fenced in by something substantially stronger than chicken wire. The cage suggested squash but it was by no means big enough. The agent told me that she did not know its purpose and then, as if to distract me, said that the Osbornes had been fond of Rome and had planned the flat as a *pied-à-terre* for future use. I could only imagine that they were taking no chances against the happy day, and that if it was to be dampened by a visit from an idiot grandmother, they would be prepared. Well, if worse came to worse, so could we be. The Osbornes were beginning to irritate me anyway, with their fancy ways and wonderful servants, and I thought that our Luke could be chained up there just as well as their old grandmother.

When we had retraced the six steps between the upper terrace and the lower drawing room, the agent, as she had promised, asked if any of the three was free but, alas, it was as she had predicted. One man was already in service and had come only for this day to help his former colleagues with the finishing touches. The woman, whose name was Vigi and whom I had eyed with particular greed, was promised to a Lady So-and-So, a special friend of Mrs. Osborne, and was therefore out of the question, although her life, as she implied with perfect *bella figura*, would henceforth be virtually over insomuch as she couldn't accommodate *il signore*. The other man, Alfredo, was even more dramatic. He was promised to the Belgian Ambassador but he was very unhappy about it because, said he, "The Belgian Ambassador has eight cars and it is a known fact that he kills his drivers." "Then," I asked, "why do you go?" Well, he had been promised by Mrs. Osborne, it was as simple as that. "You see", said the agent, "he has given his word". "So," said I, "have I." It was at this point that the agent repeated verbatim my initial proposal. By good luck it struck all the proper notes of *bella figura*, for it implied largesse, that is, that I wasn't going to haggle over the price of the flat if I could get what I wanted and of course what I wanted was altogether flattering. It pleased them all but it delighted Alfredo, who laughed and said that he would like to speak with *il signore conte*. I said that I was no count but that I should be glad to speak with him anyway, and we fixed the appointment for an hour later at the hotel.

I came back to the hotel feeling terribly pleased with myself. At such moments perhaps it is the eternal child in us all that again seeks praise, but, whatever the reason, one is particularly vulnerable to wifely criticism. In fairness too, on the so-called adult level, it should be remembered that my wife and I had experienced enough disappointment to promote edginess. In any case, we who seldom bickered, had an awful row. Pamela said in no uncertain terms that I was a blithering idiot, that I had gone out to find a flat and had come back drivelling about a manservant, that we couldn't afford a manservant to begin with and probably no servant at all if we didn't immediately get out of the hotel, that with two small children it was madness to employ a man without knowing anything about him except my hunch (note both the hostility and chauvinism: as if men were by nature more pernicious), that I had gone off the deep end just because someone had called me a count, and anyway, if we wanted a manservant (ah-ha, feminine illogicality!), what was the matter with Francesco. Francesco was an old crook whom the concierge had dug up – prior to the interlude with the Jeanne Eagles nurse and before the tropical rains had set in – and who, after Pamela and I had completely gone to pieces at the prospect of again feeding a duck, had on occasion consented, for an enormous fee, to drive the children to the park. "Francesco," I said, "is a thug." There was no arguing this but there was also no arguing that the children each time had been returned to us, at least insofar as the naked eye could see, intact. "Besides," Pamela said, "Francesco speaks English. Does this man?" I said I doubted it. "In that case," said she, "what am I supposed to do with no Italian?" "Learn it." In this happy manner conversation continued until the phone rang to announce Alfredo.

He was announced punctually on the hour and this impressed Pamela even though she was not generous enough to admit it. Alfredo, however, as he came in, was less subtle, for he couldn't conceal his amazement at our grandeur. Nor could I with his. To describe him as the Prince of Wales had looked in his youth would be misleading, for Alfredo is Italian, short and dark. But he was dressed similarly. His blue suit was not serge nor cashmere either but something so exquisitely smooth that it could have been spun only by underwater nuns in some distant tropic sea. And the cut! All, indeed, was perfection except that his collar was worn and frayed. Against the otherwise epitome of elegance this fray was not only reassuring but actually endearing. He immediately endeared himself too, for when Luke, by way of greeting hit him in the eye with a baseball (Italians can't catch, the national game being soccer), he said, "I have children of my own, *signore – è normale.*" Now in Luke's short life people had loved him for his beauty, for his wit, for his individuality and doubtless, as in the case of other handsome bad-men, for that hidden sweetness that the infatuated always egomaniacally hope to bring out, but in the same room never had the word normal been contemplated, much less uttered. This time Pamela could make no pretense of indifference and, as if by way of gratitude, took the children away.

I asked Alfredo to sit and he deferentially sat. I asked what his work had been for the Osbornes. He said that he drove, that he was an excellent driver and that of course he took care of the cars (the inference being obvious that I also had a stable full). He served at table; *la signora* Osborne, he said with pride, had taught him and so he could do it very well. He drove the Osborne children to school, he called for them and on the nurse's day off he helped to take care of them. He cleaned the floors and did all the heavy work. He cleaned the shoes and took care of *il signor* Osborne's clothes. He shopped, except of course for food, which was the province of the cook. But otherwise he bought everything. He said, this time with tremendous pride, that *la signora* Osborne had trusted him with millions, and, in point of fact, it was he who had paid all the bills in the *Via in Caterina.* He said he arrived at eight and stayed until work was finished (which must have been late enough if the Osbornes were fashionable, for even ordinary people begin dinner after eight). He said of course he was given *da mangiare.* He did not sleep in as he had a wife and children. *La signora* Osborne, he said, had given him a motorcycle to commute with.

I asked him what *il signor* Osborne had paid him. He took a deep breath and said, "Forty-five thousand ($73 per month) and that's the holy truth." Now although salaries in the last few years have risen, this was not so out of line, for even if housemen of sorts can still be found for around thirty thousand, they do not also drive. But all Italians, as I knew even then, love to bargain almost as much as they love to exaggerate and certainly "the holy truth" was redundant and therefore suspect. But then why had he taken the deep breath, for an Italian can top Scheherazade any day without bothering to bat an eye? All things considered, it is likely that he thought he was in the presence of a *selvatico americano* – an American wildman – and hiked his price accordingly. But on the other hand and against circumstantial probability, I believe he took that breath because, suddenly face to face with a *selvatico americano*, he had wildly decided to risk all on the truth. Of course I shall never know what Mr. Osborne paid him. But I knew, whatever the amount, he was worth more, and so I in turn took a deep breath and said I would pay him 50,000 ($81) monthly and, if all went well, add 5,000 ($8) monthly each successive year until death do us part.

Alfredo sat there. Was my offer so magnanimous that he was overcome? Or had I botched it, somehow unknowingly, offending his sacred *bella figura*? As it turned out, I had been right about his "risking all", for he was considering it, but not in the sense that I had imagined. For finally, slowly, emotionally he said, "Look, *signore*, I am a serious man. I do not run around *in cerca*; I have a wife and two children and I love them. I do not want to work for the Belgian Ambassador. I would like to work for you. I would work well – you can ask anybody. But you have just arrived and you are a foreigner. What happens to me if you don't like it here and go away, for example, in three months?"

There had been my hunch and now, the more he spoke, the more I felt it was confirmed. I really wanted this man because I felt that with him somehow our unfortunate beginning would be smoothed over into a happy time. But fair's fair, and so I said, "What you say is true. It is our intention, however, to stay for several years. We plan to put the children in school and it is not easy to change schools every few months. But there is a certain risk in life no matter what you do. You have to make up your mind and take a chance on me just the way I am taking a chance on you. I cannot guarantee anything. I can only give you my word that we intend to stay. I have always wanted to live in Italy. But I cannot promise to remain here on account of you."

"Certainly," Alfredo said and smiled. "I will take the position."

"When can you start?"

"Now, in an hour. I must get my uniform."

He was back on the dot, uniform correct although happily, like the collar, a little worn. Meanwhile Pamela, in her joy at the prospect of a home, seemed to have forgotten Alfredo or at any rate her reservations about him. In any case she lost no time in using him, for they immediately left to meet the agent and make an inventory. There are always inventories and they are very tedious. Every scratch is noted.

Pamela returned with more than the inventory. There was the light of love in her eyes. I mean neither to stress nor deprecate the natural pleasure a woman feels when working hand in hand with a young, handsome male, but love is composed of many strands and one strong one unwinds back to long ago. Long ago, in another Southland, Pamela had had a nurse who later became what was then called "a personal tweeny", and the fact that this loving, faithful servant was both of the same sex and different colour made no difference, on the contrary perhaps it made the sudden cross switch possible. In any event Pamela had found what she had lost, and Alfredo, in turn, had found another Signora Osborne, different certainly, obviously less fashionable and, therefore, according to his book, odd, but kind, and most important of all, unquestionably a "*signora*". It was love, mutual and wild, at first sight. From here on I was permitted to have the services of Alfredo on my birthday and once, when I was grazed by a motorcycle, he was allowed to drive me to a first-aid station, but otherwise, according to the rule in our family, I was automatically rated fourth, for naturally the children also fell in love with him. Of course at this initial stage Pamela did not know this. Not that she any longer really cared. She was far too gone. To save face she said, "It remained to be seen how Alfredo would work out with Luke and Rachel." But otherwise he was a genius. He was a wonderful driver, "Why, I was even relaxed in Italian traffic." He was courteous and as quick as lightning. In no time at all they had packed away all the expendables in packing boxes that Alfredo, apparently out of nowhere, had produced. When I asked where in *that* flat they had found place to store packing boxes, she said there wasn't any place, Alfredo had gone out and brought back some men to cart them away. He had helped with the inventory, laid and lit the fire, checked the frigidaire, made the beds, swept the terrace, gone out to buy coffee, tea, sugar, pasteurized milk and other essentials, and then, *en route* back to the hotel, he had taken her to a special shop to buy shredded wheat. Now shredded wheat in Rome is very hard to come by, let alone the difficulty of describing a food product that, to Italian eyes, is unbelievable if not also insane. I was extremely curious to know how Pamela, who only a few hours before had been proclaiming her ignorance of Italian, had suddenly managed to translate "shredded wheat", and so I asked if by chance Alfredo used the Berlitz method. Pamela haughtily replied that she was not a complete nincompoop, that after a month in Rome she had picked up something of the language, that anyway Alfredo spoke a little French, and that after all language was perhaps not so important as I imagined, or in any case it wasn't insofar as Alfredo was concerned, because he was altogether intuitive. As if on cue Alfredo arrived to demonstrate, for, without any visible means of communication that I could see, he began taking down suitcases and packing and, more marvellous still, when he came to that one French dress near which none of us was allowed to breathe, he skirted it as if it were the holy of holies, bowing to Pamela and thereby indicating that this shrine for all loveliness was not intended for rude albeit willing hands but for her inviolable touch. They worked with such wonderful synchronization that although I wanted to ask if we were moving immediately in spite of the elements, for it was cold, raining and dark, an interruption would have been an intrusion. But there was no point in asking. We had moved.

Moving for the first time from a hotel into a home abroad is like graduating from high school, for life is supposed to begin again in a new world filled with mystery, adventure and wonder, all plugged for direct contact. In a sense this is true and yet it is also make-believe, because just as an adolescent will continue to be an adolescent for some time if not also for life, so we continued to be foreigners and strangers. Nevertheless there is the fact of graduation – in our case from the tourist class – and with it a fine feeling of accomplishment. Moreover Alfredo allowed us to explore this new world, for, in addition to all his other attributes, he was a genius with the children. Every hour on the hour he locked them away in the cage on the terrace. In that hour he cleaned, shopped, went to the *questura* for the *permessi di soggiorno* that foreigners must obtain every three months (he got ours for a year), found pamphlets about schools, complained to the agent about functioning cats and the non-functioning elevator, in short, everything. On alternate hours he unlocked the cage and took the children to the zoo. At the zoo he personally knew an elephant, an old friend called Romeo, who, for one peanut, when you said, *"Su, Su"* would stand up and when you said *"Giù, giù"* would come down. The probability was that Romeo, having gone up, would have come down anyway, but this was irrelevant, because when a child first discovers that he can command several tons of living flesh to do his bidding, a sense of power is released that makes the world irrelevant. Moreover, Romeo had a wife, Giulietta, but she was flighty; sometimes she would go up and sometimes she wouldn't, and, as her infinite variety gave the game zip, the promise of her favours became the perfect bribe. On account of it the children went to bed when Alfredo said it was time for bed, they stayed in bed until he arrived in the morning, they played the games he thought they should play, they ate what he gave them to eat.

What they ate and, for that matter, what we ate was no problem, for shredded wheat can be disguised in many ways. But Alfredo wouldn't touch it. Nor would he go near the stove. None of us for a moment believed that he couldn't also cook, but he said that he couldn't and the reason that he said so was of course on account of *bella figura* and, as we found out later, in deference to a very fine point in that meticulous code. It was not that the act of cooking would have been against it but the fact that he was working for people who didn't also have a cook would have been very *brutta figura* indeed. Pamela sensed something of this and she tried, but she is of the chafing-dish school and besides her heart wasn't in it, because what had really persuaded her to come abroad and live in Rome had not been so much the wonders of the eternal city as the promise of a cook. Alfredo was of course extremely polite about her offerings but they were obviously not to his taste and, worse still, they upset him perhaps emotionally even more than digestively, because according to the code it was wrong for his signora to be in the kitchen at all.

We had put off finding a cook only because our faith in Alfredo was so great that we believed that he could eventually persuade Vigi to come. But finally, when he could stand it no longer, he said, "Look, *signore*, Vigi would like to come more than anything else in the world" and so on endlessly *alla bella figura*, "but honestly she cannot. She is engaged." There was no alternative then but to send Alfredo off to an employment agency, instructing him first to try for a dwarf, an unnecessary stipulation really, for it was obvious that our little flat could barely hold another soul. We did not then know that Roman employment agencies are notoriously unreliable, nor that Alfredo was incapable of intelligently employing anyone, for, although like all good servants, he identified with his employers, being Italian, he also so identified with the unemployed that he could refuse no one work. This was of course all in his moral favour, but it was of little help in finding a cook. In any event there were no available dwarfs and apparently, from his efforts, no woman who had ever before seen a stove. What these women ate at home I cannot imagine, for with us they couldn't even cook *pasta*. Even worse, when a domestic servant is abruptly dismissed, a reasonable amount of room and board must be paid in addition to two weeks' salary. In consequence I cannot believe that during this period either the Roman police or the public charities had much of a problem with female delinquents, for most of them were on my payroll. This, in all fairness, distressed Alfredo. It distressed him even more that he was starving.

Then one day the miracle happened. In walked Vigi, suitcase in hand, all smiles, "If you want me," she said. She said furthermore that she was no cook, she had been Signora Osborne's lady's maid but she had always worked in good houses (*bella figura*) where she had "seen how it was done", and she would help out until we found someone. "How had it happened?" we asked Alfredo. "Well," he explained, "Vigi had been very unhappy with Lady So-and-So, who had only given her an egg to eat." Or maybe it was a grape. The words are confusing to newcomers: *uovo* means egg, *uva* grape, but the plural of egg is popularly *ova*. Anyway, egg or grape, it was absurd because there is always pasta. In retrospect, I now think it must have been a grape, because eggs can be of great importance if not also a mark of esteem in Italian life. In the old days and sometimes even now, as I have the misfortune to know, if you went to a peasant's house, he would of course give you a glass of wine. This is simple, courteous *bella figura*. But if you make a particularly good impression and he decides to do you real honour, he will say "*Il signore* will take an egg?

A fresh egg?" From the noise outside he seemingly extracts it from the hen; in any case it is brought to you fresh with mother warmth and it is very *brutta figura* to refuse this singular honour. But it is hell to accept it, for the egg is chipped open in front of you amid smiles of delight, love, international affection et al, and you have to gulp it down raw. Now Vigi had been and was still at heart a country girl. Furthermore she had a kind of neurosis about eggs or anyway the great moment of her life had evolved around the spilling of one. We knew about this almost immediately because at bedtime she told the children stories and among them her favourite was *Come io ho tolto la macchia dalla ball-gown della Principessa Torlonia* (How I took the spot out of Princess Torlonia's ball-gown). Like all these stories it did not begin with *once upon a time* but *in the happy days when I worked for Mr. and Mrs. Osborne*. In those days of course Mr. and Mrs. Osborne did not live in a little apartment like this. It is ludicrous to think of such a thing. They lived in a great house on the Aventine hill and in that house they had many parties with all kinds of wonderful people, princes and princesses, counts and countesses, grand and beautiful ladies all dressed, needless to say, in exquisite ball-gowns. One of these parties was especially gay and lasted until very late, indeed until the morning, when Mr. and Mrs. Osborne decided to serve bacon and eggs. With the bacon and eggs there was, needless to say, more champagne. In the hilarity, Princess Torlonia spilled her egg on her new, exquisite, satin and jewelled Parisian ball-gown. She was *mortificata*. Signora Osborne was *mortificata*. Vigi was *mortificata*. Everybody was. So Vigi took Princess Torlonia into the *guardaroba*, think of that! (The *guardaroba* is a room in every respectable Italian home where the servants eat, washing and ironing is done, and things are stored or guarded.) Vigi helped Princess Torlonia out of her dress and then Vigi took a great risk. She used a concoction, the secret of which had been handed down to her by her grandmother, who was a witch, put it on a damp cloth – *O dio*, if she had ruined the gown! – and out came the egg. A hot iron, needless to say, was always ready and waiting in the Osborne home. Vigi took the iron and, placing the damp cloth between it and the dress, pressed the wrinkle and dampness away. You couldn't even tell where the egg had been! Princess Torlonia was delighted; Signoria Osborne was delighted; everybody was delighted. Vigi never got over it.

We could hear every word of these stories just as everything else could be heard in that flat and Vigi knew that we could hear them and so, while telling the children about the Osbornes, she would tell us what she wanted us to know. She would pause, as it were for station identification, and say that Alfredo and she knew that we couldn't stay on much longer in such a little flat, or that until the signora's clothes came (sic) she would happily take care of the few that were already there in addition to cooking, or although she had had a room of her own at the Osbornes, she didn't mind temporarily using the divan in the discreet gentleman caller's (upper) sitting room. It was an insidious business, this oblique attack, but at first we were so happy to have Alfredo and Vigi that we paid no attention to it. They were happy with us too and yet, on account of Vigi's makeshift quarters in the upper sitting room, we almost lost them both at the start.

One night shortly after Vigi's arrival, on our return from dinner at a nearby restaurant, Pamela couldn't find her pocketbook. She couldn't remember whether or not she had taken it with her but we both quite definitely thought that we had seen it in the flat. Nevertheless I went down and searched the car, and then together we combed our thirty square feet. We thought that Luke and Rachel might have borrowed it to play Princess Torlonia calling on Signora Osborne or vice versa; they took turns as it was more fun being Princess Torlonia because you were allowed to spill. We went through all their junk and although I recovered my *permesso di soggiorno*, no pocketbook. We thought that perhaps Vigi had been playing too, for she often joined in as Princess Torlonia or *il signore* Osborne or even as the last of the Italian kings; she had a moustache and was terribly good at male impersonations. It was then that I made the great mistake. I climbed the three steps to the upper sitting room, and, after looking around, got down on all fours to look under the bed. Vigi was an old maid who prided her virtue. But she was also slightly deaf and I didn't think she would wake up or, in the event that she did, I knew, historically speaking, that I wouldn't be the first Roman master to have approached a servant's couch nor, for that matter, the first to have made the pass on all fours. Nevertheless, Vigi's awakening was rude and my position, looking up from under the bed, humiliating. *Brutta figura*. In the confusion I made the horrible mistake of blurting out that I was looking for *la signora's* pocketbook. God is my witness that I never suspected Vigi, that I suspected my own flesh and blood, to wit, Luke, and that Vigi's room was the last place I had thought of looking. All to no avail. Vigi was *mortificata*. She was worse than that: she was heartbroken. She wept long and loud and would listen to nothing.

Our hope was with the dawn. But when Alfredo arrived, to our great surprise, he was extremely upset too. He said he had been *in servizio* with Vigi even before the Osbornes and that she was altogether honest, otherwise he would not have recommended her. I had had no sleep on account of Vigi's sobbing and perhaps for that reason I was not my habitual angelic self. In any case, I yelled at Alfredo that "no one was questioning Vigi's, his or anyone else's honesty." Alfredo was hurt by the tone but impressed by the volume. He went out and began yelling at Vigi. This in itself was not unusual; on the contrary, in certain spheres it is apparently a male prerogative; but the substance was different. He said Vigi shouldn't be a fool; he said that the *signori* were foreigners and didn't know any better, that they left everything lying around so that it was enough to make an honest man want to steal, but anyway, *pazienza*. He then returned but it was the old impasse: loyalty to master and loyalty to his own kind. It was also the beginning of his first sulk. He took a dim view of Vigi's staying. He took a dim view of telephoning the restaurant. Yes, he would condescend to telephone but he knew of things having been lost in *that* restaurant before. He took a dim view of people who carried all their material goods around in a pocketbook, for it had contained, in addition to American and Italian currency, my wife's passport and American Express checks, the crown jewel, the children's first pictures, in short everything. He took a dim view of reporting the loss to the insurance company, he had little faith in insurance companies. "Besides," he said, "That would mean reporting it to the police." "Well," I asked, "what was the matter with that?" "Oho," he said, "that would be the end of me, and Vigi too, altogether." It was an ultimatum but it was a great deal more than that because he said it so emotionally; apparently he felt that honour, *bella figura* and all that was good in life would be forever lost if his name were entered on a police report. But he was straight about the alternative because he added, "Look, *signore*, I am terribly sorry about the pocketbook, but I know Rome. You will never find it."

For two days Vigi wept. Alfredo sulked and we wavered. It was an unpleasant situation because, although we had never suspected Alfredo, from our point of view or even from our mores, we would have thought that he would have wanted it reported to the police and so out in the clear. Besides, in addition to a substantial loss, it seemed insane to have this loss covered by insurance and then not to claim it. But on the other hand there was another value: we recognized the potential loyalty and devotion of both Vigi and Alfredo, we knew that we should never find such people again, and we knew too, if we reported the loss and even if they stayed on, everything happy in our relationship would be gone. But it was not a simple choice because the question was, if we didn't report it, could we feel good about them or, if something should again be lost, what then would happen?

On the third morning, while we were still sulking, weeping and wavering, I went out to get the car. As always it was parked in the nearby Piazza Farnese because the French Ambassador lives in the Palazzo Farnese and the police, who guard his slumbers, also supposedly keep an eye on the cars. A kind of somnolent, half-closed eye, for many mendicants always spend the night in the cars parked there. All apparently own, if nothing else, a set of keys to any car and there appears to be a pleasant, unwritten pact that governs procedure. The mendicants, for their part, only clean the cars out of cigarettes, lipsticks and sundry incidentals. They never take car papers. On the one occasion when I left my keys in the car, they took the key-ring together with a very nice St. Christopher medal but they carefully left the keys visible in the pocket. It seemed fair. The early morning ritual is that you come to your car, the policeman turns his eye away. You knock at the window, looking pained and severe. As you unlock your car and roll down the window for the needed airing, the mendicant looking not so pained, just weary with no visible emotion at all, unlocks the far door of the car, gets out and walks away. Later, across the piazza, he or she lights one of your cigarettes.

On this particular morning, the ritual being over, I was about to start the car when a policeman came over, saluted and asked if I had lost anything. I thought this was strange, for they never bother about *un povero uomo*, and even though we had thought of nothing but the pocketbook for two days, at that moment it never crossed my mind. So I began casually looking through the pockets. "No," he said, "I don't mean there." "Well," I said, by way of conversation and about to drive away, "Two nights ago we lost a pocketbook, a lady's brown pocketbook." "I found it," he said, "here outside the car. It's in the police station across the way." He saluted and left. I went over to the police station, identified myself and was given the pocketbook. Nothing had been touched. I took it up to the flat and amidst laughter, rejoicing and *commozione*, Alfredo said, "You see, *signore*, I told you we Romans were honest and that you would find the pocketbook."

A few weeks later Alfredo, who was ordinarily very cautious, while shopping left the car unlocked and a package that he was to have forwarded to Mrs. Osborne was stolen. He was terribly upset and kept saying, "I can't understand it. I don't know what happened." But we knew what had happened. His old allegiance was finally over, for we had trusted him and not gone to the police, and he was henceforth no longer *la signora* Osborne's man but ours.

What we didn't know was that we were also henceforth his. Perhaps we should have been aware of what was happening, but the *bella figura* line, even though insistent, is indirect. Yet the handwriting was on the wall if we had only read it, or, more precisely listened to it, for Vigi, in telling the children her *Tales from the Lives of the Great*, always told us which way the wind was blowing. The wind, after this incident of the pocketbook, abruptly shifted: the attack on our little flat was temporarily dropped and, instead of stressing the Osbornes' magnificent house on the Aventine, she took to emphasizing their many cars, and she would pause to say, "Alfredo thinks it's a great shame that your father hasn't his own car because when Alfredo is taking you to school or out shopping, your poor father has to walk" or "*Diamine*, the other day Alfredo saw your father get on a *filobus*!" or "Yesterday Alfredo was heartsick, seeing your poor father go out in the rain." Now I had always liked going out in the rain or thought that I had, and in Rome I not only enjoyed walking but I loved the *filobus* particularly the two marked either ED or ES. ED is for Esterno Destro (External Right) and ES is for Esterno Sinistro, and these two creakily meander around the city, not so externally either, for they more or less hug the ancient walls, and riding them is a pleasure because, besides seeing the city and its people, if you stay on long enough you can always get a seat and, if you miss your stop the first time, the car eventually circles back for another chance. But the power of advertising, as Vigi well knew, is in its insidious repetition, and so of course, finally, I began to feel sorry for myself.

About this same time too our car, for one questionable moment, was highlighted in Roman fashionable life. It was a Volkswagen bus, and at first Alfredo had been happy with it because, in comparison with most European cars, it looked big and it was shiny and at that point there were no others in private use around Rome. What happened was that we had friends who had friends who had a box at the opera, and our friends' friends went away and gave them their box. In consequence, for three weeks running, we were invited to the opera and our first appearance was on opening night. Opening night at an Italian opera is a kind of combination of the World Series and opening night at the Metropolitan. Everyone knows the names and numbers of all the players and the arias too and everyone is dressed to the teeth and so were we. Likewise of course Alfredo. He was shined up to kill and as happy as a lark that his *signori* were going to the opening. Because our bus held nine people, we had offered to call for the whole party and we did. They looked pretty good too. En route there was some pleasantry about the car but nothing untoward, on the contrary mostly compliments about its convenience. But when we pulled up at the opera, there was a riot. The head doorman thought we were delivering the milk and didn't want to let us drive up. But Alfredo out-screamed and out-emoted him and for a moment I thought there would surely be bloodshed because all the way to the opera Alfredo's *bella figura* had been over-sized and then there was this terrible deflation. Yet the incident with the doorman was as nothing compared to the excitement when we actually drove up. Dowagers were squashed and lorgnettes broken as we piled out of the milk truck. Poor Alfredo was *mortificato*.

But he was confused afterwards because, due to another confusion, a kind not uncommon in Italy, there had been a mix-up in boxes, a very pleasant one as it turned out, and in consequence we came out of the opera with the British Ambassador in tow. Not only that, but the Ambassador got into our car, admired it and whisked us off to a marvellous party at the Prince and Princess B's. Terribly good *bella figura*, the very best. Alfredo was impressed. So was Vigi when he told her. She was so impressed that we were served the kind of breakfast that we had been trying to get all along, for Italians cannot understand anything about breakfast beyond *caffe latte*. We had orange juice packed in ice, bacon and eggs just like that night at the Osbornes, toast, jam, honey and all kinds of things. And so beautifully served. On hot plates, which is another thing that Italians cannot at all understand. For a week this went on and for a week there was no talk from Vigi about cars. But the following week, when we went to the opera, we did not come out with the British Ambassador nor were invited anywhere. The wind shifted back : Vigi talked of nothing but cars. Well, you can't listen to the same thing all over again forever, and so I bought another car.

Cars, however, did not solve the opera situation, for although our going to the opera had certainly pleased Alfredo, it made Vigi ecstatic. She would press and purr and run around like mad and say *"O elegante"* and rush out and ring for the elevator that hadn't run for two months and swear at it as if, because we were dressed up for a change, it should suddenly function, and pick lint off my coat and rush back for a comb to touch up Pamela's hair and beam and wave and oh my. We went to the opera for those three weeks and then we weren't invited any more. No more breakfasts, no more hot plates, still pleasant service but casual, a let down in tone and a general air of disappointment. So one day Pamela said, "Vigi does so much for us besides cooking and doing all the washing and ironing. She's a wonderful seamstress, she makes all the children's clothes, and she's so devoted to them. It seems to me, as it makes her so happy when we're dressed up, that we could" – "Go to the opera every week !" "We wouldn't actually have to go to the opera," Pamela said. "Alfredo needn't have to drive us, now that we have the little car, and we could just go to the movies." "I'd feel a fool," I said, for except on special occasions no one dresses in Rome. "We could sneak in late," Pamela said, "and sneak out early. You don't like movies anyway, so it all fits in. It's the least we could do for Vigi." So we did. We still do, regularly once a week every opera season, and the service is superb.

We did a great deal more. We moved, to one of the most elegant palaces in town because Alfredo *per caso* – by chance – knew the *amministratore* who *per caso* told Alfredo of an apartment that *per caso* could be had at a great bargain. In a way it was a great bargain, I suppose, for endless sixteenth-century rooms with beautifully painted ceilings cannot be reckoned in filthy lucre. But there wasn't any furniture and, on account of the rent, there still isn't. Nevertheless, this novel arrangement – our empty grandeur – has, except for Pamela and me, innumerable advantages: the children, as they ride their tricycles through frescoed rooms, are both culturally and physically in splendid condition, and Alfredo's and Vigi's *bella figura* is *ottima* for we now have four in help (the proper, discreet minimum), our address is impeccable, all the other tenants are nobles who not only bow to us when we meet on the stairs but, last Christmas, some of them deigned to enter our empty halls for carols and cheer. On this occasion, to be sure, we almost lost Alfredo, for I thought he would surely burst as, swollen with *bella figura*, he announced *"Sua Eccellenza* this" and *"Sua altezza* that". Yet the strange and wonderful thing is that, in spite of his passion for pomp and circumstance, his tenderness remains untouched. He still dresses the children every morning and takes them to school, and then he rushes back to dress us so that we get off to work on time; and at night, similarly, he tucks the children in bed and then tucks us in too. Of course we have no privacy, none whatsoever, because we belong to him. It is almost incredible. For example, not so long ago, I experienced a sensation that made me think that I should see a doctor, but, in order perhaps to avoid seeing him twice, I thought it might be sensible first to have an analysis made. I did the necessary, wrapped the bottle in paper, and told Alfredo to take it to a laboratory. "Are you ill?", he said, as if about to faint away. "No," I said, considerably annoyed, because I thought that in this one department I might be allowed a little privacy. "Just take the bottle where I told you to take it." He tried to conceal his emotion, as one does with a child, and with admirable control left the room. The next day he returned with an envelope sealed in a manner suitable, I should imagine, for papal bulls, and, after formally handing it to me, stood back at attention across the room. I broke the seals and perhaps frowned for there was the usual Latin hodge-podge. Even so, the report wasn't too hard to make out, for there was a column marked *anormalità* and this column was fortunately blank. But although it had taken me no more than a minute to decipher it, Alfredo couldn't stand the suspense. He wanted me happy as he had been made happy, for from what he said it was obvious that before the envelope had been sealed, he had discussed its contents in every detail with the technician. "Why," he said, "there's nothing the matter with you, *signore*, nothing the matter with you in the least."

126

I guess there isn't, for the price of affection is always more or less at the expense of privacy. It's just that the values got mixed, for our original purpose was simply to see Italy. But even though, on account of Alfredo and Vigi, the simplicity is gone, perhaps through them we see Italy in the best possible way. We are, it is true, hardly ever allowed to meet Alfredo's family because it wouldn't be *bella figura* for us or for them, yet we know everything about them and discuss his children's problems daily as he does ours with us. And at the time of the last Belgian mine disaster, when Vigi's brother was at work there, we put in the long-distance call because Vigi, on account of some kind of inborn feudal respect, could not be persuaded to use *i signori's* telephone for something so unheard of as an international communication, and finally, when we got through and Vigi's brother was all right, we cried for joy together in the guardaroba (just like the Principessa Torlonia!). In thinking of Princess Torlonia I think of the Osbornes and wonder about them, for now all my spleen is gone. I wonder if they too weren't once simple people and if that grand house on the Aventino had any furniture in it at all?

After Geneva

Pamela came down the hall as Jaimie opened the door. "Jaimie! How did you get here?" and she kissed him. "We were going to meet you later."

"I got the earlier plane."

The terrace door was open and the afternoon sun caught the glasses on the table. They were set out with bottles and the ice bucket.

"Who's coming this time?"

"I don't know really," and she laughed. "I wouldn't have asked them if I'd known you'd be back, but maybe you'd like to meet them. They're friends of . . ."

"I wouldn't, Pamela. Where's Rachel?"

"She's resting."

"Why? Is anything the matter?"

"She was out rather late."

"Where?' '

"I don't know . . . somewhere with Roberto."

Jaimie looked at her.

"Oh Jaimie, for heaven's sake. He's very protective. He's a darling boy and he adores her."

"I never heard that was a handicap."

"Are we going through that again the minute you come home? I can't bear it. You look all in."

He sure did. He had caught sight of himself in the mirror. He was going gray but it wasn't only his hair and moustache; his face was gray-ish too. It shouldn't have surprised him after what had happened but he was continually surprised by signs of his own age and he was surprised even more because he looked angry, angry with himself.

"Come on in and I'll make you some coffee," and he followed her into the kitchen. "It must have been awfully hard, Jaimie. How's

Felicity?"

"She's dead, Pamela."

"Oh no. How terrible. How could it happen?"

"It was too late for an abortion, but she wanted it. It was all arranged anyway. I think she wanted to die really."

"How awful . . . for Grace and Walter."

"I don't think they care."

"What an awful thing to say."

"At least one of them could have come with her."

"When Walter called he told you why they couldn't, that Grace was ill . . ."

"Oh come on, Pamela. Anyway it's not what I think. She told me."

"What?"

"That she'd always had the best clothes and the best schools and that was it. No love all the way down the line. She knew why they weren't in Geneva with her. They cared about their position, not about . . ."

"When did she die?"

"Early this morning."

"Did you call Walter?"

"Yes."

"Is he coming?"

"Yes, now."

"I'm surprised you didn't wait for him."

"I'm surprised I went."

"Why?"

"It's the old story, isn't it? The crock of gold or the rainbow, running around for some other man's daughter when I've got my own to take care of here."

"You sound as if I'm incapable."

"I don't know what the word is . . . not interested enough."

"How can you say such a thing?"

"You didn't know where they were last night."

"For heaven's sake, Jaimie. She was home at one. What do you want her to do? You send her to the French school without a word of French and she was perfectly miserable there before she and Roberto became friends. She told you herself it changed everything for her. Don't you know what a boy like that means to a girl?"

"You're confusing your feelings with hers."

"What do you mean by that?"

"You promote him. I've warned you before. You kiss him whenever he comes in the room. It comes to the same thing as not knowing where they've been : the go-ahead."

Pamela flushed. She had taken to wearing beige outfits; as they were planned for her pale coloring and sleek blond hair the flushing seemed aggravated. "We live in Italy, for God's sake. I embrace all of Rachel's friends. The trouble with you is you're jealous."

There was always a modicum of truth in what she said and she was clever. Her tactic was to turn the argument but it was pointless after what he'd seen. Still, he hadn't come back to argue nor to condemn her; he was doing it badly, so he began again.

"Look, Pamela, I should have said 'we' weren't interested, not only you, because it holds for me too. Otherwise why should I let you always persuade me about Rachel and accept what you say? You don't know what I saw. It wasn't one poor girl; the clinic where I took her was filled with them."

"How old was Felicity, Jaimie?"

"Sixteen."

"Well, there you are. Besides the difference in age, look how Felicity was brought up . . . she told you herself. After what you've been through, of course you're upset . . . who wouldn't be . . . but don't lose your perspective. Rachel isn't Felicity and, don't forget, Felicity didn't have you for a father."

It was the old flattery pitch. It was in her blood, the southern charm, never facing any unpleasantness.

"If you're so concerned, why don't you talk to the principal . . . what's his name . . . at the Lycée?"

"What good would it do? I'm talking to you, Pamela."

"What do you suggest we do?"

"When the plague comes, there's only one thing to do."

"What?"

"Run."

"Run away from one boy?!"

"One boy's all it takes."

"But there's been nothing untoward. Rachel's not going to be pregnant. I can guarantee that."

"How can you guarantee something you can't control? Anyway it's not only a question of pregnancy, as grim as that would be. Rachel's too young."

The bell rang.

"She's more mature than you think."

Had she been pleading for the boy she couldn't have put it better. She wanted them to make love, not that she was aware of it, that she was identifying with Rachel, but there was no point in telling her because she would never admit it.

"She's not at all mature emotionally, Pamela. It's unfair to ask her to handle it at her age."

"Do you think it's fair, when they're so in love, for you to decide for her?"

"Who else can? She's a child, Pamela. We don't live in India. What does she know about love at thirteen?"

"She may never find another boy like Roberto. You'd better think about it again, Jaimie. If anything should happen to him, she may never forgive you." She stood up and her eyes filled. "Besides, this is her home now. She has her friends here; she's on the honor roll at the Lycée. That's quite a feat, coming there so late. Would you take everything away from her in one fell swoop?"

Although as always there was some truth in what she said, she was again identifying with Rachel, in the last analysis thinking of herself. For she didn't want to leave Rome; she loved everything about it, the position she had made for them, being big fish in a little pond until they'd practically become three-starred like the Sistine Chapel or so it seemed from the number of people who came to the house. He could hear the last batch in the hall. Vigi had answered the bell and was showing them out on the terrace.

"You don't have to see them if you don't want." She started out. "But if you see Rachel, don't tell her about Felicity."

"Are you still telling me what to do about Rachel?"

He drank his coffee. It wasn't easy. He'd assumed, naively, that the effect of what he'd seen would be as shattering for Pamela. One thing, though, that she had said was true: there had been no indication of anything specifically sexual. But wasn't it crazy, to wait until there was?

"Daddy!" Rachel hadn't seen him either. She was opening the ice box. She was small and in her bare feet and had to tiptoe to find whatever she was looking for. "What are you doing here?"

"I live here, remember?"

She kissed him. "When did you get back?"

"Now. Are you hungry?"

"No." She put back what she'd taken out and giggled. Her dark bangs, more often immaculate, were ruffled. She seemed flushed too. "How was the girl? Was she pregnant?"

"How do you know about it?"

"Mommy said she was in trouble. What else could it be?"

"There were a lot of girls in trouble. What's that on your neck?"

"Oh, Roberto did it. We saw a man in the movies put his lip-mark on a girl's neck and he wanted to see if he could do it. He did it very well, didn't he?" and like a child pleased with a tracing, she lifted her neck to show him. She was so unaware of his reaction that he controlled it. "I wish you'd have been here earlier. Roberto's little brother was here. You should see him, daddy. He's a little Roberto . . . the same big black eyes and hair."

"How old is he?"

"Eleven. He's darling."

It occurred to him that she was nearer Roberto's little brother's age than Roberto's. "How'd he happen to come here?"

"Oh, we were at their house and he wanted to."

It was the first time that Jaimie had heard of her going to his house. "I want to speak to you about Roberto, Rachel."

"Not now," and she giggled again.

"Why not now?"

She didn't have to answer. "Rachel," the voice called from the stairs. "What's keeping you?" and then Roberto appeared. "Oh, signore, I didn't know you were here."

"I didn't know you were here either. Where were you?"

"Upstairs." He looked at Rachel. "We were studying."

"In Rachel's room?"

"Yes, signore."

"Are you in the habit of going to girls' rooms? Or is it because you have no respect for Rachel?"

"No, signore."

"Then why do you bite her?" Coming out with the word released his anger. "Are you an animal in a zoo? Or what?"

Rachel laughed. It calmed Jaimie down. "Why don't you say something? Do you know why I went to Geneva?"

"Yes. Rachel told me."

"I went to see one girl who was pregnant but I saw many more, I don't know how many. None that I saw was as young as Rachel, but I thought about her all the time, and about you too, Roberto. I don't suppose any of the boys who were responsible ever meant to have those girls there. But that doesn't help. What do you think will happen to them? What kinds of lives will they have? I can tell you what happened to the girl I went to see: she died. And I'll tell you something else . . . maybe I shouldn't say it. It wasn't only the fault of those boys and girls, or not to begin with anyway; it was their parents'. And this parent hasn't seen his daughter for three days and I'd like to. Have you any books upstairs, Roberto?"

"No." He was a big handsome boy; all through Jaimie's lecture he had been looking at Rachel, but now he looked at Jaimie and smiled. He thought he'd got off lightly.

"Well, then . . ." Jamie got up.

"Thank you, signore."

"No, Rachel, I'll take Roberto out," and at the door Jaimie went outside with him.

"Haven't you your bacho this year?"

"Yes, signore."

"Then you won't be a boy anymore, but a young man. In fact you're that already. With a young man's problems and desires. Rachel's too young for you, Roberto. You have no right to put your problems on a girl of thirteen. She hasn't them yet, and shouldn't have, and without you won't have them for a while. That's why I don't want you to come here again."

"Oh, signore." The big boy wasn't a man at all. He began to cry.

"Are you that fond of her, Roberto?"

"Yes."

"I don't believe you. You're crying because you can't get what you want. Did you ever stop to think what she wants? I don't think you ever did. You went to the movies to mooch around in the back seats and to her room to kiss and bite because you've got hot pants. Let's be honest about it. You're going on eighteen. All right, find yourself a girl of your own age."

"I didn't know you cared so much," Rachel said when he came back. "What did you say to him?" and she came over and sat on the arm of his chair.

"What makes you so sure I said anything?"

"Oh come on."

"I told him that he had no consideration for you, that he only thinks of himself, and that when you're older he can see you if he wants but meanwhile he was not to come here any more."

"Well, that wasn't very nice of you . . . without telling me first. It doesn't make much difference, though, really, does it?"

"Why?"

"Won't I see him every day at school?"

"We're going away."

"When?"

"Tomorrow."

"Where?"

"Vienna."

"Oh poor Roberto. He really loves me, daddy."

"What makes you think so, Rachel?"

"Mommy thinks so."

"Did she tell you that?"

"She didn't have to. He says it all the time. 'Ti amo, ti amo, ti amo.' "

"Is that love? How do you know, at thirteen, what love is?"

"What is it then?" She was fine featured. Her delicate neck, except for the red mark, was smooth and perfect. She held it forward, taut and still, listening so as not to miss a word.

"It's what people make of it. When they're ready they can make it beautiful and sometimes lasting too. But if they start too soon . . . well, you don't put a little horse, a thoroughbred horse, in a race before he's ready because if you do he's spoiled, he can't run later or he can't win anyway. You're not a little horse, though . . . you've got more in your head and a heart too. They've got to be got ready."

"And?"

"And what?"

"Tell me more. What happens if they're not?"

"They miss out. Children not so long ago used to be sent to work

134

before they were ready, and then afterwards they were finished at twenty or thirty or anyway long before their time."

"It's not exactly the same, though, is it?"

"Almost."

"What'll Vienna be like?"

"Oh, there's wonderful music ... concerts, operas, everything."

"What'll I do about school?"

"There's a Lycée there."

"I'll never find another boy like Roberto. Why do you smile? He's such a superior person."

"What's so special about him?"

"He just is. All the girls at school are in love with him."

"Is that why you like him? You're vain, honey. You're flattered that he likes you."

"That's not all I like about him."

"I know it isn't. You're curious about an older boy, about sex."

She smiled. "Is that wrong?"

"It's wrong too soon. You've got to wait a little while, that's all. Now you tell me what you like about him."

"I like his voice. It's like velvet. Do you want to know something funny?! When we go to the cinema, he doesn't look at the pictures much. He opens his eyes very wide and looks at me and blinks. Why does he do that? Is that sexual?"

"If it is, I never heard of it. It sounds to me as if there's something wrong with his eyes."

"Maybe there is. He doesn't wear glasses, though. I think it's sexual. He knows a lot about sex."

"Oh."

"He gave up prostitutes for me."

"How do you know that?"

"He told me. When they lived in Algiers and he was fifteen his father took him to one of those houses. He's very close to his father. His father wanted him to go to the best place, you know, so he wouldn't get a disease. So he must know quite a bit."

"I don't believe a word of it."

"How can you say that?"

"Boys talk big. He wanted to impress you, and arouse your curiosity and make you think he'd had experience so you'd feel safer with

135

him. He's not the only boy ever to try that. I don't believe it about his father either."

"Why?" Her voice was very small. She had believed every word the boy had told her.

"Everybody knows there're diseases all over Africa. He certainly wouldn't have taken him to one of those houses. He's a big liar."

She didn't say anything for a while. "That girl in Geneva, how do you think it happened? Do you think she made love all the time?"

"I don't know. Why?"

"Roberto didn't just talk big."

"Oh."

"He showed me his penis. He wanted me to touch it."

"Did you?"

She shook her head.

"What else did he do, honey?"

"Isn't that enough?"

"I think so."

"He wanted to do more though. He wanted to kiss me down there. What's the matter with you, daddy? Are you so innocent? Everybody knows that. I didn't let him anyway. I couldn't; I wasn't prepared. I hadn't had my bath."

He felt a great glow of affection and kissed her, thanking God that he hadn't stayed on to meet his friend but had come back to where he belonged and was wanted. "He never let you alone, did he? Well, it's over now, isn't it, honey?"

"Yes." She sighed. She was relieved too. "In Vienna, will you be with me more? This is the first time you've ever talked to me like this. When I was little, you used to put me to sleep and tell me stories. If I'm still supposed to be such a child, why don't you still do it?"

"Would you like me to?"

"Yes." She got up. "How can you, though? You and Mommy are always with people."

"I needn't be."

"If I ever find another boy, even if he is a liar, I hope Mommy doesn't kiss him all the time. She always kisses Roberto whether I'm there or not and makes little bird noises. Why does she do that?"

There was laughter from the hall. Pamela was showing the people out.

"She always has to be the centre of attention."

"Well, she is. Why do you agree with her, though, all the time, daddy, even when you think she's wrong?"

"I do when you're around, Rachel, because I think it's better for you if we act together."

Rachel shook her head. "No, it's bad for me because she always says things that are good for her, not for me."

"Oh here you are," Pamela said, coming in smiling. She was elated. People were like drink to her. "They were charming. You should have come out and met them. But no matter, we're meeting them for dinner and then going . . ."

"We're leaving, Pamela."

She had her back to him, emptying an ash tray, and turned. "When?" It was more than a question.

"On the first plane in the morning. Perhaps you'll spend this last evening at home."

"What are you ringing for?"

"For Vigi. She can begin packing."

"Shall I take all my books?" Rachel started out. "All of them?" But she didn't seem interested in her books.

"I would. But you don't have to pack this minute. Why don't you stay with us, honey?"

"No," and she left.

"You see how she feels about it."

"She's not upset about leaving. I think she's relieved. Or anyway she wasn't upset until you came in. Maybe she is now because you are, but that's something else again."

"You put everything on me."

"I think she left because she didn't want to hear us quarrel."

It was the first time he had real misgivings, not only about whether or not Pamela would come, but about the effect on Rachel if they split up. That was a lesson from the Geneva book too: Felicity's parents were forever quarreling and splitting up and coming together again.

"You know better about everything, don't you, Jaimie? What I resent is that you blame me, that you think I'm incompetent, just because I didn't happen to know where they were for a few hours last night."

"What about today?"

"What about it?"

"Do you know where they were?"

"Of course I do. They were here with his little brother, Marco."

"They were until Marco left. Then they were upstairs in Rachel's room. You didn't even know he was in the house."

"Maybe you'd be better off without me, Jaimie."

"I'd be better off without the traffic in this house. We'll do it differently as far as Rachel's concerned, that's all. From now on I'll be with her more."

"How, if you're away all day?"

"I won't be. I can work most of the time at home."

"May I ask where that's going to be, or is it asking too much?"

"Vienna."

"I might have guessed. You've been wanting to go long enough. I'll say one thing, you're persistent. Oh God, Germany. Well, it's the same thing, they talk German. I can't leave in a few hours. No one could."

"You don't have to come right away. Think about it and come later. You didn't want to come here, remember? Maybe you need a little vacation. But come, Pamela, if not for me, for Rachel."

The doorbell rang. Jaimie was beside himself; he thought Roberto had come back. He was almost right. Vigi announced his father.

"It's not decent to those people not to show up at all. I'll say good night to Rachel and then go for a while. I need to get out of the house for a little anyway."

Jaimie had seen Signor Bara at the French school. He was head of the maths department. All that Jaimie knew about him was that he and his family were of Italian origin and had lived in Algiers and left when the French pulled out. According to Rachel he had been a professor there and his position at the school in Rome had been a comedown for him. He had looked older than Jaimie imagined perhaps because he stooped.

"You will excuse the intrusion," he began politely and then shifted gears. "My boy took my razor blades. He wanted to kill himself."

He expected Jaimie to say something but Jaimie said nothing. He was looking through a crack in the door; it was not properly closed and he could see Pamela's dress.

"I've had a long experience with the young. I know something about their affections and sorrows but I know of nothing like this. Of course this is my first experience with an American family . . ."

"Excuse me, Signor Bara. Why don't you come in, Pamela?"

She did. She had not before met Signor Bara.

"Signor Bara is angry because I told Roberto not to come back here."

"He tried to kill himself, madame."

"Oh, how terrible. I was afraid that . . ."

"May I ask . . . and you too, madame, now that you're here . . . is it customary in your country to give young girls complete freedom, to go to the cinema with a boy late at night or to his house or wherever they wish and then abruptly, without warning . . . and for no reason, he tells me . . . shut the door in his face?"

"Oh come Signor Bara, there's a reason and you know it."

"Oh I know the reason. Where we lived, in Oran, as in every respectable Arab community and for the same reason, girls are kept behind locked doors. It's considered backward. Perhaps it is. But at least, if I may say so, it's responsible behavior. If Roberto had done anything . . ."

"That's what I said too, Jaimie."

"But he didn't. I know my son. He would have told me."

"Did he tell you that he told my daughter how you took him to a brothel?"

"I beg your pardon?"

"I didn't know that," Pamela said. "Why didn't you tell me?"

"There's quite a bit more, my dear, but why should you be exposed? You're entitled to my protection too . . . As to our being irresponsible, Signor Bara, it's true; we were. But if your son took your razor blades so that you knew he took them, it doesn't sound as if he intended to use them. I may be wrong, but it sounds to me as if he wants more of your attention. Why then aren't you with him now instead of coming here to get your anger out on me? And you spoke of affection. If your son had enough at home, why at seventeen does he become so involved outside? Perhaps it may be easier for him, Signor Bara, after we've left. I didn't tell him . . . you tell him, after we've gone . . . we're leaving tomorrow. Are you going out, Pamela?"

"Yes."

"Perhaps Signor Bara will go down with you."

But Signor Bara didn't go. He seemed stunned. "Don't take her away," he said.

"Signor Bara, what are you saying? Are you suggesting that I sacrifice my daughter to your son? Don't be absurd. He doesn't mean anything to me. I'm sorry you're distressed, but aren't you really blowing this up out of all proportion? Before you know it, he'll see another girl . . ."

Signor Bara put up his hand. He couldn't take any more. He sat down and took off his glasses and put them on again.

"He may not see another girl," he said. "My boy's going blind."

"Oh no," Pamela said. "It's not possible."

"He doesn't know it yet."

"But you can't be sure."

"Alas, I am sure, madame. It's a rare disease. When it comes, it comes quickly. The prognosis is for now. His grandfather, my wife's father, went blind. We don't know much about it, he died very young. We've done what we could. There isn't much we can do."

"You mean with doctors here?"

"In Oran and here."

"But they know so much now and do such wonderful things. There's a doctor in Madrid . . ."

"In Barcelona, madame."

"My cousin went to him. She came from America. He's supposed to be the best in the world."

"I know. I've written to him. It's a long expensive treatment. It has succeeded but rarely does. I believe there's an operation, perhaps two. How could I send him? And if it fails? He shouldn't be there alone."

"I will send him," Pamela said. "And go with him too, if no one else can."

Signor Bara got up. "I said some things in anger . . ." but he couldn't finish. He kissed Pamela's hand and left. He seemed more bent than ever.

When Jaimie came back from the door, Pamela was sitting with her head in her hands. "I don't think I'll go," she said. He didn't know if she meant to Barcelona or out. "Poor Roberto. Life's so unfair." She had been crying and looked up. "It changes everything, doesn't it?"

"How?"

"There's no reason to leave now."

"Just once, Pamela, why don't you think about your daughter? It's very strange, you think about everyone else, with great kindness, imagination even, but not about your own family. Why is that? What do you want her to do? Feel guilty or devote her life, beginning now at thirteen, to a boy who's blind? She shouldn't know anything about it."

"If I go to Barcelona, she'll find out anyway, won't she?"

"Are you going? Why? Are you planning to take up with him where she left off?"

"Do you care if I do?"

"I know my limitations, if that's what you mean. I can't compete with a boy of seventeen."

"Do most people have such rotten thoughts, Jaimie, like you?"

"What do you see yourself as, Pamela? Why don't you come out of that Lady Bountiful mist? Why else would you go? They don't need you. All they need is the money and you've promised them that. Where you're needed is where you belong . . . with your daughter."

"Well, that's a surprise. From the way you talk I would have thought I did her more harm than good."

"That's right, you do if you don't think about her. Did it ever cross your mind how she would feel if you went to Barcelona? She resents you enough already for kissing him."

"She does no such thing."

"You remind me of the lady who told Freud she never dreamed. Do you know what he said? 'Too bad.' She would hate you for the rest of her life."

"You don't love me any more, Jaimie."

"Yes, I do, very much, but I won't accept your judgement about Rachel any more. Because you haven't any. It's a defect, we all have them, mine was in thinking that you had. I wanted to leave a year ago but I listened to you. Roberto's a bastard, if you want to know, with a thirteen year old girl, but if he hadn't come along, someone else would have. It's in the air we breathe, an Italian with a foreign girl. But you didn't see it. You don't even see now why we should leave. You never even saw what was happening here."

"At least I was here. You weren't. You were always in your studio. Working all day? Not from the stories people told me about who came to see you. It's very easy to put the blame on me and you're very good at it. You were very good with Signor Bara too."

It was the same old tactic, but the difference was that this time what she said was true. He was about to tell her that he knew he was to blame too, perhaps more so, for hadn't he foreseen what might happen and what had he done about it? Nothing until . . .

"I promised to meet those people and I'm going to keep my promise. Whatever I do is wrong anyway. Good night, Jaimie."

He heard the front door close and then Rachel and Vigi laughing upstairs.

Dear Katie

Dear Katie,

How many extensions are there on that phone? And does every-body listen in? As to your young cousin being impressed with the length of my calls, the quality of the drawing (the gallery people messed it up by the way, it was supposed to have been waiting for you on arrival) and the wonder of my having chosen that particular dress – the precise color to set off your skin and hair – you might tell her that there was no wonder about it, that I know every shade of your lovely skin and that the dress was absurd anyway because a body like yours shouldn't be covered at all, although I suppose you cannot walk out naked even in the Boston heat. Your precocious little cousin gives me a pain in the ass and I suspect she's in back of your aunt's taboo on telephoning. Yes, I know your uncle's ill, but it's hard going not being able to call you. It's worse than that – we've not spoken since the divorce came through!

I have my ticket for the 14th and reservations, in both our names, at the Ritz. I can't wait. I'm a free man at last – but not for long – we'll marry right away and before you know it, well, maybe not ac-tually before you know it, but soon we'll have that baby we both want.

You were right to refuse your friend's house, even though we'll be legal. Why be burdened with that set up? We'll find a sublet some-where until your work's finished, maybe in Cambridge, Brattle Street used to be lovely and it's not so far from your hospital. And afterwards let's take a trip. Neither of us has ever been in Japan. Or what about France? Isn't there some place near where you were brought up? You always speak about it with affection – I'd like to go there with you. In any event somewhere beautiful for prenatal influence, or don't they believe in that anymore? We'll show them. Any place you choose will be fine. And after that, well, this letter is about after that, I've been carried away.

While writing this I suddenly wonder why, as you love France so much, we never considered settling for Paris? God knows there's no language barrier and child analysts are in demand everywhere. Does this surprise you? It does me a little.

I know we'd taken for granted that we'd live in London and that's still all right with me, but not in this house, please. For the last two days, since the divorce came through, I've been looking it in the face. I know you like it – I still do in a way – but it's too loaded for obvious reasons. No, let's give it to Rachel and start out fresh.

Yesterday morning, in gratitude although a year late to be sure, I sent Natalie flowers and wine to Jean-Marie, and then later I ran into them! Although I hadn't named you on the card, Jean-Marie didn't miss a beat. He immediately spoke of the party and repeated word for word our conversation when I first saw you, in white, at the top of the stairs and asked, "Who's the girl?" and he said, "Which?" and I said, "There's only one." Anyway they asked where you were and I boasted, at length, telling them that you were now a fully-fledged child analyst with your own seminar at the Boston conference and about your imminent work at the hospital. Natalie is strange about you, darling. When I told her about the divorce, she said, "It's a great responsibility, your having met Katherine *chez nous.*" "What kind of a remark is that?" I said, "I'd think it would make you happy" and she said, "It will if it makes you." What happened between you two? Should I ask her what she meant?

Also yesterday, while waiting at my osteopath's, I read a piece on Australia's Great Barrier Reef. I think I'll do a children's poem about it. On account of the color it should be illustrated by a first-rate painter, although it's strange, with all the hullabaloo about art, the U.S. never prints a handsome book for kids. It's for our baby of course. Not every child has a poem written for him before he's conceived. It's called *The Teddy-Bear Fish* and begins,

It's beyond belief
The Coral Reef
Come see
What's under the sea.

As you start down
There are coral crowns
For seaweed of maidenhair
That floats in the breeze
Of the tides underseas
Purple and gold and brown.

As the further you go
In the fathoms below
Where the magic of colour is found
The water is purer
And deeper and bluer
Here deep-sea fish swim around.

There are big fish like whales
And small fish like snails
There are catfish and batfish
And some are called hatfish
With feathers that float from their tails.

There's a fish with a face like a clown
There's a manta or ray
That just likes to play
And urchins and squirts
That squirt til it hurts
And a fish that lives upside down.

They wear red like in fires
And blue star sapphires
And orange and scarlet and gold . . .

And so on. Do you like it? As a newly ordained child analyst I value your opinion. I hope there's nothing significantly wrong. Squirts til it hurts perhaps?

I love you,

JAIMIE

Katherine darling,

Your letter surprised me. First and least, there's no need to delay coming on account of the book. The proofs came as advertised and I'll be finished in good time; in fact, I may come a day early. If so, I may beat this letter but I write anyway. Later, dear, surely if we try hard enough, we can find something better than the house for misunderstanding.

It is not primarily because of Rachel that I suggested giving it to her. It is because of you. For if it had been the other way around, if you had been married, I'd want none of it, that is, a house in which you'd lived with your husband. Don't, please, again read between the lines because there's nothing there. I've spoken little of your predecessor, not because of any effect or feeling of guilt but, on the contrary, because she doesn't interest me. You do.

Do I hear you say, "But you had so much resentment, Jaimie?" Of course I had when she was so ornery in delaying the divorce and, as a matter of fact, I still have on account of Rachel, because her mother became a very foolish woman and it cost Rachel more than perhaps meets the eye. I would have separated long ago except that then Rachel would have gone to her mother – legally, and that would have been the end of her, of Rachel, I mean. As it turned out she solved it herself, or the first step anyway, by marrying so early. I'm sure she married, in good part, to get away from the tension and I always thought Alexi, although there was never any doubt about his loving her, married to get away from home too. Well, although it may not have been according to the book, it worked out because now, as you remarked, she seems just as much in love, if possible, as Alexi is.

All of which is a detour that leads back to the house. Because when Rachel married – she was seventeen, Alexi barely eighteen – she wanted to go on using the studio and so I put in the separate entrance and the window for the proper light. Perhaps she wanted to see what the house would be like without her mother in it or maybe she was too young for a complete break. I don't know. All I know is that I was trying to give her, not her lost childhood, but the childhood she never had or its security. It would be wrong now to take it away. It would be just as wrong for you Kate, because she would resent you. And if we didn't, it would be worse. The studio would become a watchtower. How could it be otherwise with her mother's successor? And what chance then would we have to be relaxed and happy? It would make good material for a play or a story – I may write it but I don't want to live it. It's too risky. That's why I wrote let's give her the whole shebang and start out clean.

By the way, she and Alexi phoned from Sparta yesterday. It must be boiling, but they sound happy so I suppose it makes no difference. When I told her about the divorce she said, "Now you can marry Kate, daddy." I said, "I plan to but it takes two to make a bargain" and she said, "Oh, come on, she's perfect for you." You are.

JAIMIE

Kifissia

Dearest Kate,

I might have been with you in Boston now or by tomorrow. I guess there's something the matter with me, even at a time like this, always to be wanting you.

After writing you the other evening – I'd just come back from mailing the letter – the phone rang. From the ticking and the empty sound I knew it was long distance and I hoped it was you. Then the voice said, "This is the British Consul in Athens. I'm afraid I have bad news for you" and the world stopped turning or rather I could feel it go on endlessly turning, not caring. "There's been an accident. Your son-in-law is critically hurt and your daughter's been hurt too." "Badly?" "I don't know how badly" and he gave me the name of the place and the telephone number and name of the hospital and the doctor's name. It was a strange Greek name and I wasn't sure I'd got it straight. All I could think was: this isn't the time to go to pieces. So I repeated the information but I still wasn't sure about the doctor's name, Ioniadis. Then I made a mistake: I asked him, in the event that I couldn't reach the doctor, that he phone and ask him to stay there and get whatever other doctors and nurses that might be needed. He asked me if I wasn't British and when I said, "No, American" he lost interest.

The long distance operator said there was a six hour delay to Greece. I said, "Oh no, that's not possible" and my tone convinced him. When I told him what had happened he got me through in ten minutes. The doctor, thank God, spoke English. He told me that he thought now Rachel would surely live. He'd just left her. He'd been with her for three hours. He said Alexi's condition was very critical . . . "While there's life there's hope" but he wasn't his patient. He said he was going home. I said, "Oh no, please don't" and my tone must have convinced him too, for he asked, "Why? Do you want me to stay?" I told him that I'd never wanted anything more, that it was awkward talking about an honorarium but that I would do anything he wanted and please to tell this to Alexi's doctor too. He promised to stay until I came. When he asked when, I said I didn't know, I'd take the first plane. It turned out that, except to Paris and Milan, which was no help, there wasn't a plane until the morning.

Then I tried to get Rachel's mother in Baltimore but there was no answer. Since I changed lawyers and pressed the divorce we'd never communicated and I had no idea where she was.

It must have been about 10 : 30 by then. I called Eliza – you know, the woman I always wanted you to meet. She and Eric, her husband, have more sense that I have or anyone else I know for that matter. Besides, they're fond of Rachel. She said Eric would prepare a kit of homeopathic medicines – he's not a doctor but he's a wizard with them. She said, "Let me think. I'll call you back." She called back right away. She said, "Jaimie, this is the time to get a private plane." I said, "How?" but she didn't know. She said, "Try the airlines, or what about your fancy friends?" The airlines were no help. I called Ian and got his Chinese boy and jibberish. Then I called Lady T. and Constance, both of whom said, "Oh, darling." That was a great help too. When I asked Constance about Roger Clarke – she's a friend of his – he has a private plane – she said, "Roger never did anything for anybody in his life." I didn't say what I thought.

The one person who might have helped I hadn't thought of – yes, Jean-Marie. He said he'd come right over. I again said, "Oh no," but with less success. So I said, "Look, Jean-Marie, that's not what I want. I want a plane. And I have to keep this phone open."

It was only then that I realized that I hadn't called Alexi's mother. I thought, "Oh God, I've got to call Tamara." I did but there was no answer in the Hague. Then I remembered that she had gone to their place in the Saltzkammergut above Ischl. She and Oli, Alexi's stepfather, had been married for twenty years – he'd brought up Alexi and loved him very much – but last year he left her for his secretary. Alexi used to joke about it, but underneath he was upset, for whenever his mother telephoned to ask what she should do and then when Alexi wanted to do something, such as speaking with Oli, she wouldn't let him. She always said the same thing, she didn't want to burden Alexi with her troubles but now that he was gone and married she was so alone. And now!

Then Eliza called again and asked about Rachel's mother and Alexi's. She suggested I wire to all addresses and say it was urgent and they both should call her. As it turned out Alexi's mother couldn't come. Rachel's arrived yesterday.

Jean-Marie called back. He said there was something called Europe Assistance in Paris, that he talked with them, that they couldn't get a plane here until the morning – on account of a landing permit – and even then they couldn't guarantee the time. So that was that. Then I tried to call you but no luck. Maybe it was just as well this time, darling, that I couldn't get you, I might have broken up but I so wanted to hear your voice. I still do.

Later

The plane left at 9:30 and I was in Athens at 2. At the airport and in the plane I tried to pray that if Rachel were too badly hurt she wouldn't have to live but I couldn't bring myself to it. I didn't know how to pray anyway. Even so I tried to make a pact with God to give him everything I had if only Rachel would be all right.

I asked the stewardess to find someone to get me through customs and she did, a girl who told me where Kifissia is – forty minutes out of Athens. She got money changed too. Fortunately I had a lot of currency and I had Eric's medicine in my briefcase. I didn't wait for my bag. She sent it after me.

My driver was a killer. As we wove in and out of streetcars, he casually glanced at the oncoming traffic, as if the cars were so many flies, unpleasant but inconsequential. I had a ride like that once before, in Dubrovnik, and I wondered if the farther east one goes, the worse it gets, until in India, perhaps, with its fatalism, they don't even bother to look. And then suddenly I felt sick, thinking about accidents being purposeful and Alexi and Rachel in this traffic. Neither of them drives well. Hadn't they cared? Or don't kids care anymore? Or maybe they never cared in the excitement of tempting fate even right here long ago when, in the chariots, they tempted the same fate with the shears. And then, just then, over the dirty buildings, I saw the Acropolis. All my life I'd read about it and I was kind of saving it up, for my old age, maybe, and there it was, less than nothing.

The hospital was streamlined, a compound of new white buildings. Later I was told it was an accident hospital. They were expecting me in what I guess was the reception, where there was a friendly man who spoke Italian. Then another man came who spoke English. He said he'd been Rachel's anaesthetician. He said he thought she'd be all right now. When I asked him about Alexi, he shook his head. He said they hadn't told Rachel how bad he was, they'd told her he'd been taken to another hospital. All this on the way to Rachel's ward. Dr. Ioniadis had gone to eat something. But they put a white coat on me and let me in.

It was an intensive care ward but I didn't know that then either. You remember how badly I felt last Christmas when you took me to see your children in that hospital? Well, this time I guess I was hysterical. I thought Rachel was in the first bed but I wasn't sure. I didn't want to mistake my own child so I looked at the other beds, five of them. Her head was bandaged, there were bandages under her eyes, she was swollen and bruised like a fighter and talking to herself as if in delirium. "Hello, honey," I said and took her hand. She started and then opened her eyes and said, "Daddy, what took so long?" A nurse gave me a chair. "Oh, honey," I said again and she kept on saying "Daddy". Then I began giving her the medication Eric gave me. There was no problem about her taking it because she'd been brought up on Eric's doses, and, in her helplessness, the feeling of going back to baby-hood care must have been reassuring. Anyway, she kept repeating, "Daddy" and I wondered if when little children fall and hurt themselves, they are so frightened because they too think that they've almost died. Then very quietly she said, "You're hurting my hand." I'd been pressing it as if to give her my strength and it was all blue and bruised. "Oh, honey," and I kissed it and put it on mine and held it there until the doctor came. He wanted to speak with me and when I told her she nodded.

He took me down the corridor to his room. He said at first he hadn't been sure he could save Rachel, she'd come in collapsed and was cut all over, the worst a concussion on the back of her head, but it hadn't affected her brain because she'd given him my telephone number as soon as she'd come out of the anaesthetic. They hadn't been able to keep her under all the time, there was too much to do. There were cuts above and below her eyes but with the maquillage girls wear these days, it wouldn't show. He had reset her nose. Her left knee was fractured, in a temporary cast. There were broken ribs. "She was very brave. She never complained. She's a lovely girl." I took some bills from my wallet, put them in an envelope and gave them to him. I pretended to be embarrassed but I had done this kind of thing before. "No," I said when he thanked me, "It's I who am grateful," and this time I wasn't pretending. I told him that the envelope was only a beginning, a deposit on account and had nothing to do with the hospital bill. He said, "You asked me to be honest. One thing isn't perfect. It's her stomach. If it doesn't soften, we'd have to operate. We'd have no choice." "When?" "In a day or two. It would not be serious." "After what she's been through!" I said if possible I'd like to avoid an operation and in any case, although I had every confidence in him, I would want to call in a surgeon from London. He said he would welcome it. He was a nice man, tall, gangling, perhaps forty. He said he was tired, he was going home for a few hours sleep. "And what about my daughter's husband? Where is he?" He told me in another wing. "Can you be his doctor too?" "I've seen him. I can go on seeing him if you want but he has an excellent doctor, better than I am. I'm afraid it's not a question of doctors. Of course one never knows."

He took me to the other wing. On the way he said that Rachel had asked about her husband and he confirmed that she had been told he'd been taken to another hospital. He said it was standard practice in critical cases. "It would have endangered your daughter to tell her his condition."

The nurse at the entrance desk told him there had been no change. Alexi's doctor was on call and would be back in the evening.

As in Rachel's ward, there were several nurses. Alexi was in the last bed. Dr. Ioniadis told me he was in a coma and under heavy sedation. He said he always tried to avoid it, that Rachel had had very little, but that in Alexi's case it was a blessing.

Alexi was all bandages, breathing heavily and attached to a machine. The turban of bandages, with his pallor, made him the image of his mother. Except for a cut on his cheek his handsome face was unmarred. "Alexi," I said, "It's Jaimie." His arms and hands were in splints and wrapped with bandages too and so I put my hand on his shoulder. "Alexi, I'm Jaimie. I love you, Alexi, I love you very much. Because you're such a wonderful boy. Yes, you are, that's why we all love you so much. You'll get well. Sure you will, there's no doubt about it, there can't be, Alexi, because we love you so much. We wouldn't let you not get well. You'll be all right. You'll be fine."

I told Dr. Ioniadis that I would stay a while longer and walked to the door with him. I asked him when I could speak with Alexi's doctor and to see that there would be no trouble about my getting in to see Alexi and to leave word that if his mother came I should be called immediately. I told him he was her only child. Then I went back to Alexi and put my hand on him again and said, "Alexi, it's Jaimie." On account of his breathing I didn't dare give him Eric's tablets but I put a drop of liquid to his lip. "You'll be all right, Alexi. Rachel will be too. She has the strength to want to be, to want to get well. You have too, Alexi. You always had the strength for more than that, Alexi, to make people happy even when you were in trouble. Remember, when I came to Naples? I came because I loved you, Alexi, I've always loved you. That's why I wanted you for my son. So you can't die. You haven't got the right to die before I do. Remember Naples, Alexi? You were just as low then, yes, you were, you were desperate. And you pulled yourself out of it and made us laugh. Remember how we laughed on the plane? You always had the God-given gift for happiness, to make others happy, to make us all happy. You can do it again and keep on doing it, not for us, Alexi, for yourself. You can get well, but it's your choice – to decide to live. You're such a wonderful boy – yes, you are, such a rare person – you can do it."

I thought he tried to move and then he opened his eyes. "Why, there," I said, "You're better now, already," but although I went on talking to him and giving him the liquid, trying to encourage him, there was no response. After a while I said, "I'm going now, Alexi, for a little while. I'm going to see Rachel. I'll take her your love," and I kissed him. "I'll be back soon."

I hated leaving Alexi. On the way back I tried telephoning London from the receptionist's cubbyhole but it was impossible. I have no luck phoning, Kate, from anywhere, have I? But my friend, the Italian-speaking receptionist, sent the telegram for me that I printed to Eric, asking him to get a surgeon here immediately and what to give for Rachel's stomach and telling him about Alexi's condition and asking what I could do.

When I sat down with Rachel, she was asleep and muttering again. It was lucky about the medication, that Ioniadis was giving her so little, it meant ours would have a chance to work. I doubted that against the heavy stuff it could help Alexi. Every fifteen minutes or so, I gave it to her. To the nurses, if they noticed, it looked as if I were wiping her mouth. Sometimes she'd cry out, "Oh Alexi!" or "Alexi, the truck!" and struggle to get away from whatever she was seeing, and then I'd wake her and comfort her. Once she said, "Why did you wake me?" I don't know how long I sat there.

After a while someone tapped me. It was all in Greek but I got it – there was a call for me in the cubbyhole. It was Eric; even before my telegram arrived he'd been trying to get a surgeon, but he wasn't very hopeful because the reputable ones were all committed and there was no point in sending just anyone and he suggested getting a private plane and taking Rachel to Zürich. I told him that she didn't know Alexi's condition and would never consent to being moved without him and, that if she knew, she might not want to get well. He said it was a bitter choice and asked about Rachel's doctor. I told him that my hunch was that he was a good one and the hospital, surprisingly, seemed first-class. In that case, he said, to delay Rachel's operation as long as possible and to give veratrum. "You've got it in the kit. I know because I put it there, and keep on with the other medication, it won't conflict." "And for Alexi?" He hesitated. "You've got to face it, Jaimie. There are times when nothing can help. You've had your miracle." Then Eliza came on. She said Rachel's mother had phoned from the south of France, and was on her way, but Tamara, Alexi's mother, had fever, some kind of flu. A friend had called. Eliza had told her not to try to reach me, that she would relay information. "Although," Eliza said, "Under the circumstances that's asking a lot." "Not enough," I said, "Isn't anyone coming?" but Eliza didn't know.

While I was talking the receptionist had brought me Greek coffee with honey cakes. It was getting dark and I was afraid I'd miss Alexi's doctor but first I went back to start Rachel on the veratrum.

There was another nurse at the desk in Alexi's ward and she wouldn't let me in. While I was trying to explain the doctor came out with two interns. He said they'd done everything they could, that they hadn't expected Alexi to live this long, it was only because his heart was young and strong, and that after the heart the two essentials they always looked for were the spine and the brain and his spine had been damaged. "But his brain is all right," I said. "Well, when a patient's in a coma," he said, "There is no way of telling what cells have been affected. In his case I'm afraid we'll never know . . . although sometimes we can when they open their eyes." "But he did open his eyes." "It can happen," and he added, "If you say so," and he looked at me. "We've had the experience. We've seen the young die before. Those whom the Gods love, they say. I can promise you only that he won't suffer." I told him a surgeon was coming from somewhere, I thought from London, and I gave him the same amount I'd given Ioniadis. He thanked me and said, "If he's coming for your son-in-law, he'll probably be coming too late," and he explained that besides a surgeon there was a physician in each ward and that in addition Dr. Ioniadis had been seeing Alexi. "But if you like, I can call someone else in, not for your son-in-law but for you." I said I would and asked him to see that I could get into Alexi's ward whenever I was able to come, which he did.

When I went in to Alexi, I thought he was breathing more heavily. I spoke to him for a long time but there was no response.

On my way back to Rachel I didn't have much hope. I didn't even know what to hope. They didn't know about his brain, and with his spine injured, even if he got well, he'd be crippled. Should Rachel live all her life with an invalid? And what about him?

Rachel was sleeping quietly. I'd given her a round of medication when Ioniadis came in. He examined her stomach. He said it was no better but no worse. He practically ordered me to go with him to a cafe in Kifissia. While I ate he told me that all the papers had reported the accident. It had been drizzling and they were on a very bad curve, where there were accidents every week. They'd collided so hard with a truck that its engine caved in. There was nothing left of the car. Afterwards, when he drove me back to the hospital, he said, "You must get some rest too. I'm used to it," and he showed me a cot in his room. But I didn't want Rachel to miss the continuity of the doses and so I'm sitting here giving them to her – it's almost morning now – and writing you. She still calls out for Alexi and "The truck, the truck!" and then I pat her and she goes back to sleep.

Do you think there is something the matter with me, at a time like this when Alexi's life is at stake and Rachel's happiness too and perhaps her life as well, that I always think of you? I write on and on, pretending that I'm talking to you which would mean that you are here with me, and so you are.

J.

July 13

Dear Kate,

Rachel's mother came this morning. With two of us there will be no break in the round-the-clock medication. I told her about the night-mares, crying out for Alexi and "the truck, the truck!", and prepared her, if Rachel should ask for Alexi, that she should say she didn't know, she just came. Now I can be with Alexi more.

I just came from him. There is no change. Maybe that's hopeful. Doctors have been wrong before. Although he gives no sign, I talk to him all the time, telling him how wonderful he is and how wonderful he always was with Rachel, never asking for anything for himself, always loving her in spite of her demands, that few older men were mature enough to go on loving a girl so spoiled, that when he got well it would be different and easier, that I'd give him his own bank account so that he could choose too, they'd be even happier that way, he could go on that wonderful trip he'd always wanted to take to China. Yes, as soon as he got well they'd go to China.

I'm at the hotel. I'm supposed to be sleeping but I'm too wound up. I never needed much sleep anyway. What I need is you. Writing you is now compulsive like dope, so bear with me, Kate; it's a poor make-shift but balsam. If I could hear your voice I'd stop. I have a call in now, although with nobody speaking any known language it probably won't come through; perhaps it's the political situation that makes it so difficult. This afternoon I'm to meet with Alexi's doctor and who-ever he's called in, a heart man I think.

155

Alexi's examination was almost perfunctory. The specialist said nothing could be done, that it was a matter of time, perhaps of hours. Afterwards I sat with Alexi for a long time. I cannot understand why no one from Holland has come. Alexi was very much loved, not only by his mother and Oli but by his own father and everyone. I just don't understand it.

Midnight
Your cable came. Thank you.

Rachel has a slight temperature. Ioniadis says that her stomach is no better but no worse either and that it's strange that it's static. I spoke with Eric, who said that it sounds as if the medicine may be holding it, that we have to give it time, to keep on with it without interruption. I'm sitting here giving it every ten or fifteen minutes now. She seems hot to me.

In the corridor last night, coming back from Alexi, Ioniadis came out of Rachel's ward. It was very late, perhaps after two, and I thought something might be wrong.

"On the contrary," he said, "She's much better. Her stomach's begun to soften and she has no fever. You can relax . . . about her now. And as for your son-in-law, there's nothing you can do. I don't want another patient, *I'm* too tired, but if you keep on as you've been doing I'll have one. I think you should tell Rachel about her husband."

I told him that I wanted her to have more time, that each day she'd be stronger, that about that he should trust me as I was trusting him.

"All right," he said, "But how long do you think you can stand it? There's just so much any of us can do – that goes for me too. Come on. I've got some medicine for you," and he told me he'd been in the operating theatre for hours with a couple who were on their honeymoon.

In his office he poured two shots, big ones. "How long has Rachel been married?"

"Four years almost."

"Why so young?"

"I didn't decide it."

"Why? Was she pregnant?"

"No, they haven't a child, fortunately. I tried to postpone it by taking her away, that is, to London. But instead of a wall there was the telephone. I mean, Romeo and Juliet had a wall. When she didn't call him he called her . . . collect. I didn't know people could talk so long. It didn't help them, though. His family became worried about him, seriously; and Rachel was very unhappy . . . I don't know why we're all so stupid about young love. We know it's the time when feelings are most intense . . ."

"So young, my God," Ioniadis said. "Well he got what he wanted. Four years . . . that's more than most of us have."

"He earned it."

"How?"

"He knew how to love. He taught Rachel. I don't mean sexually. Few people love like that. I think it was because he didn't hate anybody : it was all funnelled in one direction. He loved his family too."

"His family? I didn't think he had one . . . except you."

"Oh, yes – and me too. We were very close. I can't understand why no one has come. His mother is ill, but I'm not even sure it's that. She's a very passive woman. But there's his stepfather too. He brought up Alexi and adores him. It could be that he doesn't know about it. He and Tamara, Alexi's mother, broke up last year."

"Another woman?"

"His secretary."

"His father's where . . . dead?"

"No, but he's irresponsible. I never met him. Apparently he's had children all over the place, both legitimate and illegitimate. Rachel didn't like him but she was probably prejudiced because he had a child by some other woman about the time Alexi was born."

"It's not easy after a child's born." Ioniadis poured his own drink first. "The competition's so hard. I couldn't take it either. I'm not proud of it but if my son were dying, I'd get to see him, if only to ask for forgiveness."

"I don't think Alexi thought there was anything to forgive. That was the wonderful part about him, his acceptance. He was fond of his half-brothers and sisters and he loved his father as he was. He respected him too, Peter Lendholdt – that's his father – was a kind of national hero, the youngest man – a boy, actually – in the Dutch resistance. And according to Rachel, Alexi was the only one in the family whom his father really loved. But if he doesn't come now . . ."

"It'll be too late for you too," Ioniadis said, getting up, "If you don't get some sleep now. How are you going to help your daughter if you're so exhausted? She'll need you when the boy dies. You're the one she'll want. She said so when she came out of the anaesthetic. She said, 'I want my father'. But she won't have one, sure as hell, if you keep on the way you've been doing," and he drove me to the hotel, where I'm writing you. Verbatim too. Why? Because I am exhausted and can't let go. Also, incidentally, Katie because I love you. Goodnight.

Alexi died yesterday. His father was there. Maybe Alexi waited for him. I know that long ago, when my father was dying, he'd waited for me. When I came in Alexi was breathing with great difficulty; two nurses were with him and a big, broad-shouldered man was sitting by him with his head bowed. He got up and said, "Peter Lendholdt. How is your daughter? Better than my poor boy, I hope." An intern gave Alexi an injection and they massaged his heart. His doctor came. "You were very good to him," Lendholdt said, "It's too late for me to be," and he began to cry. "He may hear you," I said and Lendholdt stared at me. "I believe they often do," and I put my hand on Alexi's arm. "Alexi, it's Jaimie. I love you very much, Alexi. Your father's here, Alexi," and to his father, "Talk to him. Comfort him." His father called him Sacha and spoke to him in Dutch but he lost control and went and stood by the window. I told Alexi how wonderful it was that he'd done everything in such a short time that could be wished for in a long, long life. After that I had the feeling that he was less and less there. In a little while he stopped breathing and it was as if he were relieved.

His father wept and embraced him again and again until the doctor motioned me to help get him out of the ward. Peter said, "I can't stand it. I lost my brother at his age. The only two people I've ever loved." Outside the doctor got him to take a pill and gave him more for later. He took me aside and said there were formalities, papers to sign, but they could wait until tomorrow, the important thing was to see that Peter ate something and to get him to sleep. I said I'd somehow persuade my hotel to give him a room – it's the tourist season – but the doctor said, "They know me there – you've had worries enough. Let me take care of Mr. Lendholdt."

"No, I want to be with Rachel's father. Let's go," Peter said and stood up. He's a remarkably handsome man – no wonder Alexi was so handsome – also his mother, Tamara, is very beautiful.

I had a bottle of whiskey at the hotel and after I'd got him a room I ordered sandwiches. He wanted only the whiskey but he ate part of a sandwich – to please me, he said – and every so often he took a pill. He told me that he'd named Alexi after his older brother, Sacha. When the Germans came Sacha had gone underground and taken him – Peter – with him. He'd worshipped Sacha, whom he'd seen killed. Peter was seventeen then and after that he'd been good for nothing . . . oh, he'd been a commercial flyer and raced cars but it hadn't worked – he was still alive. I said I didn't see why a man who'd been in the resistance wasn't worth more than a successful collaborateur, but he shook his head. He said he knew himself, he was worthless, he didn't even bother to get up anymore, that the only thing he'd ever been good for was women, they'd always liked him, they were the aggressors too, because after Sacha was killed it was as if everything had gone out of him. He'd never been in love. When he married Tamara – he was twenty – she was the most beautiful girl he'd ever seen, but beauty can get boring too. The trouble with Tamara – besides her beauty, which was all she cared about with the exception of Alexi, who'd been an addition to her beauty – he'd been an incredibly beautiful baby and together they were really something to see – was that she could never face anything. He doubted that she was really ill now, not that he blamed her, poor woman. His one regret was that he'd never done anything for Alexi and he hated to think what Alexi must have thought of him. I told him, and Peter's smile, through his grief, for that moment had Alexi's acceptance and happiness too. He said that I must forgive him, that it wasn't only Tamara who couldn't face things, he couldn't bring himself to see Rachel, that he just couldn't do it. Until then I hadn't thought about his seeing her but I was relieved, for how could he be asked to hide his grief so that she wouldn't know?

He was getting woozy and stumbled over to the bed and I said I'd go and let him sleep. "Oh no," he said, fumbling with his shoes. "You stay. I like you, Jaimie. It's not the whiskey. I'm not a drink talker. I'm not a talker at all. Do you know why I talk to you? Because you could talk to him." He got the shoe off. "No, it's not that. It's because you loved him and could show it . . . so he knew it. I could never show my feelings to anybody. Think of that. Not even to my Alexi. And now . . ." He got the other shoe off and lay back on the bed. "I wanted to, Jaimie. Oh how I wanted to, and he'll never know." "He knew, Peter," I said. "Love doesn't have to be spelled out." But he was asleep.

I sat there thinking of the terrible waste of Alexi's dying so young, and of Peter, who had never been able to show him his love, and how lucky I was, without reason, to have Rachel alive, while poor Peter could never make up for the lost chance. I don't think I even tried to get up. I'd watched Peter wash down all those sleeping pills; they must have worked on me too, for the next thing I knew was, hours later, when I woke up in the chair, I was another man, as fresh as if I'd slept through until morning. I left him a note saying where he could find me.

J.

Kifissia

Dear Katie,

We moved Rachel to a private room this afternoon. It was time because each day she became more aware of her surroundings and they were grim. Before she moved I had the telephone taken out. That was grim too because with it went perhaps my last chance of hearing your voice. There are no booths. But there was no choice because of the risk of a call coming through that might mention Alexi.

Rachel's room is ample, even pleasant as hospital rooms go, with one side all glass so that she can look out at the trees, and there's a Morris chair on which I'll sleep. But best of all there's a vestibule, with doors at both ends, that leads to the corridor. This means I have a private place in which to write to you.

For the first time Rachel asked me about Alexi. I was worried that she hadn't because of what Alexi's doctor had said about how different brain cells might be affected, although it may be, having been so close to death, that until now all she could manage was the business of her own survival, as in the ward, where at first she was oblivious to the other patients and then gradually came to know everything about them. Still it's strange, for she's very intuitive. She said, "Have you seen Alexi?" I said, "Yes." She said, "How is he?" "About the same as you are."

I've been expecting your first letter although perhaps it's too soon; if the Greek mails are like the telephone it may never come. Still, I can hope. I can hope too that it won't be long before we're together.

J.

Kifissia

Dear Katie,

We'll have been here a week tomorrow, which means, counting your aunt's curfew, we haven't spoken together for a month almost. How is your uncle? And *you*? I hope that living with your relatives isn't a burden. I should have insisted on your letting me put you up in the first place – at the Ritz or somewhere less Ritzy – wherever you wanted. I still wish you would. Don't get overtired. If your left eye is beginning to twitch, use that euphrasia I gave you – 10 drops in a half cup. Not that I mind its blinking, I find it provocative, either eye, other parts . . .

I don't know how much longer it will be. For the first time yesterday Rachel complained: she said the ward nurses were better. So she's improving. Then she asked when I'd seen Alexi and how was he. I said I thought all right, that it wasn't as easy in the other hospital, they weren't as friendly about letting me in. She accepted this for now.

Also yesterday (and to go back before the accident to where we left off, that is, about where to live) I had a long, emotional wire from Fabio Carpi saying that he had just heard about the tragedy and asking what he could do for me either in London (he leaves next week for Rio) or through his embassy here. I took him at his word and wired that I'd like his flat for a month with an option on it afterwards. You were so in love with it that night, with the terrace, the view, the plants, the Chinese boy et al. Well, they're all ours and, if we like it, we'll just keep it. By "now" I mean in about ten days when we should be able to transfer Rachel to the London hospital, although it may be sooner because I think that when she is told about Alexi we should try to get out of here immediately. I would fly on to Boston, except how can I leave her, right after she's first found out? So you come to

London, for the weekend anyway. Fabio's address is 34 Eaton Square. Everything will be ready for you. But try to make it longer please.

I know you want to see me as much as I want to see you although I really think there is something the matter with me, to plan our happiness for the exact time when I know what Rachel will have to face. I wish I could soften it. Even knowing what it will be, I count the hours until we're together because, besides loving you, I'm going to need you, for although I shouldn't complain, this pretending that Alexi is alive is agony. I hope to God I'm doing the right thing. I think I am, for the longer I can sustain it, the stronger she'll be.

Peter left with Alexi's body this afternoon. I went to the airport to say goodbye. Peter told me that he had called Tamara and Oli had answered. He could hardly talk. He said he'd come back, that Tamara couldn't make it alone, that he'd stay with her always. I wish Alexi could have known. Underneath his joking he was always so worried about Oli and his mother. Maybe he would have felt that his dying had meant something after all.

When I came back Rachel said, "Isn't it incredible that Tamara doesn't come? Really incredible."

"But she's sick."

"I think she's awful. She's never there when Alexi needs her."

"But if she's really sick."

"She wasn't sick when you went to Naples."

"Her mother was."

Rachel looked at me with something like disgust. "I think she's awful. If you were dying, you'd come."

Again:

Rachel: "You made an awful mistake."

"What?"

"You should have sent for a doctor from Zürich or somewhere."

"Why?"

"If Alexi's not conscious most of the time."

"We didn't know he would be."

She never follows through, because the logical thing for her to ask is for me to send for a doctor now. I think she's instinctively working to protect herself, I mean that she doesn't want to know but does know subconsciously. We'll probably never know what she saw in the seconds before she lost consciousness; like amnesia, it's probably too terrible to remember.

Later. Rachel asked, "Why can't they bring Alexi here? There's room for another bed."
"They can't move him."
"They could now."
"No, honey, they can't move either of you."
"I want him here. I could talk to him, daddy. It might help him. It would comfort him. Do it. Go see him now . . . then come back." It was the first time she cried, with her head turned away, with no sound, as if she'd had enough, with the pain and the pokings and the dressings and the drip, and now she's refused the only thing she's asked for, the one thing she wants.

The games are almost over. First, my pretending that you're here with me, that we're talking or rather, I'm afraid as it's turned out, that I'm talking to you. It has helped but I need more now . . . as the song goes body and soul. And as to the other fiction, about Alexi, I can't maintain it much longer – it's agony now. I'll have to tell her and then we should get out of here. As I cabled you, Ioniadis says we'll be able to leave in a few days. My guess is Wednesday. I'm a monster to think of myself but I do – which means I think of you. Well, for me, knowing that I'll be with you soon means I can do what has to be done.

I told Rachel yesterday. Before, I tried to prepare her by saying that I thought Alexi was no better, that the hospital people had become reticent. I didn't tell her then because somehow night's the worst time.

In the morning, at Rachel's request, I was supposed to be seeing Alexi. Then, when I came in, she asked, "How is he?" I said, "He didn't make it, honey," but she didn't understand and for the first time I broke down. "He never made it, honey. He was never conscious, Rachel. He never had a chance." She said, "Oh no, it's not so," meaning that I was mistaken but then she knew that I wasn't and began to cry too only she couldn't let go because of the pain in her ribs. "Poor Tamara," she said, "What will she do, daddy?" and she kept repeating "Poor, poor Tamara" and then, oh so softly, "I wasn't a good wife to him." I don't know what she meant by that, what she thought she should have been at her age. "What am I supposed to do in this empty place?" and she put her hand over her face. "Everybody's shit compared with him." It's true or almost, for Alexi never hated anyone and he never cared who people were and, more than that, although he was so young, he really knew how to love her. "He was always so good to me, even when I hurt him he never held it against me. He always forgave me;" and she went on blaming herself, for what? For having survived him? She kept on saying, "No, that's not true," as if I'd contradicted her but I said nothing until, later, I asked if she'd like to be alone and she nodded. Since then she's been quite controlled, she hasn't cried but she's so small and sad.

As I cabled this afternoon we leave Thursday. Ioniadis is sending a French-speaking intern who he says is first-rate. No answer to my cable and I've suddenly, right now, become panic-stricken. Why haven't I heard from you? Until now I took it for granted it was the mail in this God-forsaken place, but suddenly I'm very worried. Surely, I hope, if there's anything the matter, if you're not well, you'd have somehow got word to me. I hope only that I've become unbalanced with the thought of being with you so soon.

J.

London

My dear Katie,

Your letter was here when I came back. As you guessed it would be, my impulse was to go back to the airport and take the first plane to Boston, but you ask me not to and say you're decided.

I'm more than unhappy. I'm shocked, for although you write in detail about your misgivings – how you first had them when I wrote about giving Rachel the house until, as you say, they were confirmed in my letters about her from Greece – what your letter means is that my love wasn't good enough – and it's true. Otherwise you would have always known that my love for Rachel had nothing to do with my love for you.

164

I'm surprised too. Because after all our times together, I was misled by your happiness – or mine, for I took for granted that you'd be willing to share bad times too. You're still the same beautiful, bright, desirable girl for me, Katie, and I shall miss you. You just weren't ready for the "better or worse", you hadn't grown up and I didn't help you on the way.

JAIMIE